D1332054

A paperback original from *Atom* Books

First published in Great Britain by Atom 2004

Copyright © 2004 by Atom Books

Based on concepts devised by Ben Sharpe
Story by A. J. Butcher

A CIP catalogue record for this book is available from the British Library.

ISBN 1 904233 18 X

Typeset in Cochin by M Rules
Printed and bound in Great Britain
by Bookmarque Ltd, Croydon

Atom
An imprint of
Time Warner Books UK
Brettenham House
Lancaster Place
London WC2E 7EN

Before July 1st 2064, of all the employees at Solartech's Californian plant only one had ever made the national news.

Joel Shuman had been the blue-eyed boy of American athletics for a time. He'd been able to run the 100 metres like he was a blur on the track, like a special effect in a movie, leaving his opponents limping in his wake like old men waddling for their pensions. On his eighteenth birthday, Joel Shuman became the youngest man in history to break nine seconds for the hundred. His future glory seemed assured. Sadly, on the day *after* his eighteenth birthday, Joel Shuman went drinking. Then he went driving. There was an accident. One fatality. Joel Shuman's athletics career. In those days, it was still illegal to compete with a bionic leg.

So Joel's fifteen minutes of fame ended exactly on time. Tales of past triumphs and endless what-might-have-beens didn't put food in his mouth or a roof over his head, but he found it hard to get a job, more difficult still to keep one. He'd only ever wanted to be an athlete. Finally, the personnel manager of Solartech, California, who remembered Joel from fading newspaper photographs,

before the three-dimensional spreads you could get nowa-
days, hired him as a security guard. That made Joel's day.
(It also numbered them, not that anyone knew it at the
time).

Joel Shuman became just another member of the face-
less, fameless workforce at the giant Solartech plant –
people who had grown resigned to earning their pay,
living their lives and dreaming their dreams, believing that
the attention of the world had passed them by for ever.

All that changed on July 1st 2064.

It was a normal day, to start with: gossip, banter, night
shifts heading off, day shifts heading on. Plans being
made for the evening, tomorrow, next week. Small plans,
family plans, nothing the press would ever want to
know about. Plans that would never be realised.

The explosion occurred at 11.30 a.m. The first the
workers knew of it was the plant's alarm system shriek-
ing into life, like a woman threatened with a knife.
Several of them probably thought it was a drill, and were
likely quite affronted when the flames gushed through
the corridors like an orange flood and incinerated them
where they stood. Others, perhaps they with a little
latent psychic ability, must have realised what was happening, what it meant. Perhaps these had time to scream,
or to whimper, or to picture loved ones a final time in
their minds, or to reach out to clasp whoever was close.
It didn't really make any difference.

And Joel Shuman, in his uniform, at the gates?
Perhaps he ran. When he heard the roar, when he saw
the concrete shatter and the fireball flare, perhaps he ran.
He must have thought he had a chance. In his day he'd
been able to outsprint anything. But not this time.

Joel Shuman's face appeared alongside all the others on the evening news, his name listed with everyone else's.

A kind of fame had come at last to Solartech's employees. But none remained to see it.

Eddie Nelligan was not comfortable. But then, that was hardly surprising. At the present moment, he was face down in a horizontal position, suspended some six feet above the floor of a helicopter. His arms were stretched out rigidly in front of him, his legs behind, with all four limbs securely clamped to the metal spine of a contraption that seemed to be the hybrid offspring of a hang-glider and the shell of a tortoise. Further straps encircled his chest, waist and thighs, keeping him in place so that no part of his body was visible below the protective curve of the shell.

'Didn't they have something like this in the old days?' he moaned. 'I'm talking knights in armour and torture chamber sort of old days. I reckon they had these then. Not called skimmers, of course. More like the rack. This is just like the rack. Yeah,' he informed the technician who was studying the arrangement alongside him, 'and you'd have been strapping me in then with a black hood on.'

'I'm sorry, Student Nelligan,' the tech said. 'We need to adjust the tension of your skimmer just a little more.'

'Adjust? You mean tighten, don't you? Say what you mean. And how can I be stretched out any more than I already am?' The tech proceeded to show him how. Eddie felt his limbs tugged even more tautly as their confining clamps were extended fractionally further. 'Hey, that's got to be enough, right? I won't be taking out many Bad Guys with dislocated shoulders, you hear what I'm saying?'

'Quit complaining, Eddie,' sighed Bex Deveraux from the skimmer bay to his right. 'The tech's only doing his job.'

'A little pain now could save a lot of pain later,' Lori Angel added from his left.

'Oh, that's very inspiring, Lori, very nice,' Eddie applauded, his hands rather freer than the rest of his body in order to operate the skimmer's controls, set into the bar in front of him. 'Found that in the Team Leader's Book of Homespun Clichés, did you?'

'All right, Student Nelligan,' the tech finally nodded with satisfaction. 'You're set. We're all set.' He spoke into his communicator. 'Eyrie One to Eyrie Two. Eagles are ready to fly. Drop Zone in one minute.'

'Don't you just love it when he speaks like that?' Eddie said. Then the floor beneath him retracted and the parched terrain of the desert seemed a long way down and all that was preventing him from falling were the clamps and straps of the skimmer. 'You *sure* these are tight enough?' he called. The tech grinned and activated the descent mechanism. The three skimmers were slowly lowered from the helicopter and through the hatch. The wind slapped Eddie's face like a girl he'd attempted to kiss. 'Hey, Lori, Bex,' he gulped. 'You reckon it's too late to put in for a transfer?'

At the Deveraux College, many of the subjects on the curriculum were the same as any other school. Skimmer practice, however, was not one of them.

'Disengaging Eagles,' Eddie heard in his earpiece.

Liberated from their parent, the skimmers dropped from the sky and plummeted earthwards. The lyrics from an old rhyme his grandfather had taught him fluttered across his mind: 'He jumped without a parachute from 40,000 feet and he ain't gonna jump no more.'

Well, Eddie didn't have a parachute, either. But he *did* have his skimmer's velocity and directional controls.

Eddie pressed appropriate buttons. Instant response. The skimmer corrected its trajectory, transforming helpless plunge into purposeful forward motion, swooping low to the land and reminding its pilot exactly why it deserved its name. State of the art computer sensors stabilised its height mere feet from the ground, automatically adapting to changes in the topography, enabling the agents of Deveraux to streak into action at great speed and well below any enemy radar.

Eddie glanced beyond Lori to where Ben, Cally and Jake had joined them from Eyrie Two. All six members of Bond Team, approaching their targets in perfect harmony. He whooped with the sheer, raw thrill of it. 'Hey, Lori, Bex, anyone who's listening, forget what I said about a transfer. This is wild!'

A couple of skimmers to his left, Ben Stanton knew what Eddie meant. Okay, so they'd had to save themselves from certain death now and again during the past two years, but wasn't that the most exciting part of all? Pitting their wits, their courage and their skill against the crazies with mad plans who threatened the planet? And after they graduated, wouldn't there be even more danger, greater challenges ahead? Wouldn't the Stanton name . . . But Ben cautioned himself, even as he gunned his skimmer towards higher speeds, the desert floor streaming beneath him: *after* they graduated was maybe a bit optimistic, particularly for him. They'd sat their examinations last week but the results were not being announced until tomorrow. Normal classes were continuing in the meantime, if only to take the students' minds off the exams. The skimmer practice had almost done the job, but now Ben felt tension return to his muscles, a frown coming back to his brow.

Where was something to shoot at when he needed it?

'Target Zone approaching.' Lori's voice. 'Fire at will, and let's go for a high score, boys and girls.'

Ahead, an assortment of villains sprang to their feet from dried-out riverbeds or peeked from behind boulders. None of them real, of course. Training animates. They couldn't be hurt, which perhaps explained their cartoon grins and their willingness to announce their position by the ceaseless firing of automatic weapons. Not that they could inflict much harm on Bond Team, either. Any kind of hit would simply immobilise the unfortunate's skimmer and eliminate him or her from further participation in the exercise.

Eddie activated his target scanner and synchronised it with his weapons systems. Flying a skimmer wasn't too far removed from riding a SkyBike, and that was one of his strengths. 'One of?' he thought he could hear Bex sneering. All right. His *only* strength, maybe. Which was why he was going to make every stasis bolt count.

Only it didn't quite turn out that way. Not for Eddie. Not for any of Bond Team.

They started well, stasis bolts tearing through, paralysing and deactivating the front ranks of animates. But for some reason, Ben seemed to get a little carried away after that. He accelerated his skimmer recklessly, breaking the team's formation. Lori called for him to drop back but he didn't seem to hear. And he certainly didn't drop back. So then Jake boosted after him, and Lori after *him*. If the concept of luck had been programmed into an animate's brain, the terrorists wouldn't have been able to believe theirs. Out of formation, the skimmers were easier to pick off. Lori was struck first, a fusillade of gunfire freezing her controls, sending her skimmer skidding across the desert. Ben and Jake followed, as if neither of them felt like continuing without Lori.

'Eddie, we need—' Eddie never learned what Cally thought they needed. The very next second her skimmer dived into abject collision with the ground.

'Just you and me then, Bex,' Eddie observed.

'Yeah? Well don't get any ideas. I'm a dangerous babe.' She strafed half a dozen animates to prove it.

'Listen,' Eddie suggested, 'I'll watch your back while you take out the terrorists.' He veered towards Bex's skimmer.

'No, Eddie, don't get too close!'

'I'm not getting too close.'

'You *are* getting too close. If I have to make a sudden move . . .'

To the left. To avoid animate fire. Into Eddie's own flight path.

'At least we know what happens when two skimmers collide with each other.' Having crawled out from under his, Eddie was dusting himself down. 'The systems immobilise just like when they're hit by the animates' guns.'

'That is *not* a consolation, Eddie.' Bex stood close by, arms crossed and scowling. 'I told you not to get so close. So were you (a) deaf or (b) just didn't listen to me?'

'The answer's (c),' Eddie said. 'Wanted to help.' He flourished his palms in front of her. 'By the way, if madam requires assistance to shake off some of that dust, I'm here to lend a hand. Or two, if madam prefers.'

'Even *think* about touching me with those,' warned Bex, 'and you'll be in traction for a week. Don't you get it, Eddie? Your kind of help I can do without. *You* I can do without. How many times do I have to tell you?'

'I don't know,' Eddie grinned. 'You must be in the nine hundreds by now. Shall we try for the thousand?' Bex's cheeks flushed nearly as purple as her hair. 'No. It's okay. I'm joking. But come on, Bex, so are you, right? You like me really, don't you? Don't you?'

The arrival both of their other team-mates and of Corporal Randolph Keene, who'd been observing from one of the choppers, prevented Bex from having to answer. Nobody looked happy.

'Pathetic, Bond Team,' the instructor glared. 'A score so insignificant a four-year-old could count to it. You seem to be intent on sending your training into reverse and deteriorating instead of improving.'

'Sorry, Corporal.' As team leader, Lori felt it incumbent upon her to lead the apologies. The others followed suit, dutifully and disheartenedly.

'Well,' harumphed Corporal Keene, possibly relenting a little at the downcast faces surrounding him, 'let's just hope you have no need to use skimmers in the field for the time being. Perhaps it was unwise to stage such an exercise the day before you receive your examination results. Such matters can affect the concentration, I know.' Keene signalled to the chopper still in the air to land. 'Well, back to Deveraux, then. There'll be another chance on the skimmers if you graduate.'

And if they didn't? Ben felt a chill in his heart. The skimmers would be the least of their worries. If they *didn't* pass their exams, then this trip back to Deveraux would be their last.

'Ready?' said Jake. The boys stood in the doorway to the girls' room.

'As we'll ever be, I guess.' Lori didn't seem certain.

'What are you talking about? You've got a brain the size of a planet, Lo.' Jake squeezed her arm encouragingly. 'You've got nothing to worry about.'

Lori ruffled Jake's black hair. It was in its traditional tangled state anyway, so her fingers could hardly do more damage. 'Don't be so sure, Mr Daly,' she cautioned. 'I'd be fine if you were marking the exams, but the computer's doing it – and the computer's not influenced by blonde hair, blue eyes and a warm personality.'

'Then the computer's missing out,' said Jake.

'Yeah, well we'll all be missing out if we don't get moving.' Ben sounded more irritable than he'd intended. But if it wasn't enough that the moment of truth for his continued career at Spy High was, indeed, only moments away, he was still unused to witnessing open displays of affection between Lori and Daly, and they still hurt. 'The scores'll be on the screen in ten minutes, and I don't want to be marched off for mind-wiping before I at least get to see them.'

'You'll pass, Ben,' Cally said encouragingly. 'We all will.'

'Let's hope so,' said Ben.

Of course, every member of Bond Team knew what would happen to them if they'd failed. Ben had touched on the common fear of all students at Spy High: mind-wiping. At any point in the course, but particularly at finals, any student who failed to make the grade had to leave the College. However, for obvious security reasons, they could not be allowed to return to normal life with their knowledge of Spy High's true function and purpose intact. The outside world had to continue to believe that the Deveraux College was nothing more than an ultra-exclusive educational establishment. Therefore, a departing student's memories were erased, like chalk cleaned from a blackboard, and false memories implanted to replace them. It seemed cruel, perhaps, every student had felt so, but it was necessary. The integrity of Spy High had to be preserved at all costs. And besides, the Deveraux selection process was so rigorous that mind-wipes were required only on the rarest of occasions.

There'd been only one during Bond team's time at the College. Worryingly, it had come as a result of last year's finals. A second year student called Ty Brooke. Ben remembered him well. Big, arrogant. Disconcertingly similar to himself. Always bragging about what he was going to do when he graduated. Only the name of Ty Brooke did not join those of his team-mates on the electronic notice-board at the appointed time, and he wasn't slow in realising the consequences. The rule was for disappointed students to report to Senior Tutor Grant's study voluntarily and immediately in preparation for mind-wiping, one final demonstration of Spy High discipline.

Ty Brooke had decided to hell with that.

He tried to make a break for it. Ben hadn't actually been present, but he'd been told later that Ty had shoved his way through the crowd of second years, made a study elevator, made reception, was on the point of charging out of the Deveraux College itself with his mind his own. Then he'd run into Corporal Keene.

Ben was sure he'd seen Ty Brooke since. In New York City, just before Christmas. But it might not have been him. Their eyes had met briefly on a packed Fifth Avenue and there'd been no glimmer of recognition on the older boy's part. The memory still made Ben shudder. What if, one day, *he* should pass Lori or Cally or even Jake in the street and see them only as strangers?

He *had* to have passed the exams. He *had* to have done.

He heard Eddie as they entered a study elevator going down: 'Lori's brain's the size of a planet, sure, and good luck to her. I'm happy for her. But mine's only the size of one of those little pieces of rock that kind of fly around in space and then burn up in the atmosphere.'

He found Cally next to him, smiling quietly at him. He appreciated it.

The study elevator reached its destination. Deep beneath the gothic public face of the Deveraux College, this was where Spy High really started, in rooms of glass and steel: the IGC with its million electronic ears to the troubles of the world, the holo-gym, the cyber-cradles.

The notice screens and information area.

Which were quite popular, at the moment. All twenty-four second year students crammed together, forty-eight eyes keenly scanning the electronic display on the wall. Scrolling type read: 'The names of the students who have successfully graduated from the Deveraux College in 2064 will appear here in . . .' And then it gave a time-scale.

Three minutes and counting.

'So, Stanton, you nervous yet?' Simon Macey. The last person Ben wanted to see at any time, let alone now.

'What have I got to be nervous about?' Best to play it cool.

'Oh, you know, all the problems you've been having lately. Losing your girl, losing the leadership of Bond Team *to* a girl. And falling marks, so I've heard.' Simon Macey shook his head in mock mournfulness. 'I think we can wave farewell to your chances of Best in School, Stanton, don't you?' In the Deveraux final examinations, the only grades awarded were Pass or Fail, with the exception of the student who had achieved the highest marks, earning him or herself the added recognition of Best in School. 'With any luck, we'll be saying goodbye to you as well.'

'Why don't you get off Ben's back, Simon?' snapped Cally.

'It's okay, Cal.' But Ben winced. Macey had struck a nerve with the Best in School jibe. Not so long ago he'd thought that was his God-given right. 'At least there's one problem I haven't got, Simon.'

'Yeah? What's that?'

'I'm not you.'

Cally laughed. 'Hey, Simon, I'm betting Ben *is* Best in School.'

Now it was Simon Macey's turn to laugh. 'Yeah? You

reckon? I'll tell you what, Cross, if Stanton pulls *that* one out of the bag I'll run round the quad three times naked.'

'That's in front of witnesses, Simon,' warned Cally.

'It ain't gonna happen,' he scoffed.

'Forget Macey, Cal,' said Ben dismissively. 'Look at the screen.'

The seconds were ticking down and silence descended on the assembled students, tense, nervous, expectant.

Eddie: all those wise-cracks, all that larking about, but he was serious in his spycraft and he'd revised hard for these exams on the quiet. Bex: even if she passed, what if the others didn't believe it, wouldn't give her the credit she deserved, suspecting favouritism because of her father? Jake: so he hadn't had a good education like most of the others – Domers toiled in the fields, not in the schoolroom – but he was as good a spy as any of them and the results today would prove it. Lori: she was team leader now and growing to like it and if she failed she'd be relegated again to a cheerleader with ideas above her station. Cally: from the streets to Spy High, from being alone to being one of a team, all her first term doubts forgotten, there was no turning back now.

And Ben. Benjamin T Stanton, Jr. A name he thought would mean something one day. Perhaps it still would.

The seconds were in single figures now. Lori and Jake were holding each other. For once, Ben couldn't find it in himself to care. Somebody whispered him good luck.

The screen read: 'The following students have successfully graduated from the Deveraux College in 2064.' And then the names.

EPISODE SIX:

The Annihilation Agenda

WRITTEN BY:
A. J. Butcher

PRODUCED BY

www.atombooks.co.uk

for Charlotte

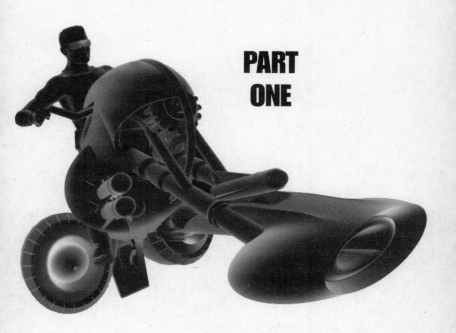

**PART
ONE**

ONE

Ben seemed inexplicably to have lost his ability to read. Letters milled before his eyes like strangers in a crowd. B. There was a B. And ENJAMIN, attached to the B which was good. Ben felt himself laughing, he felt the relief and the elation welling up inside him. It was there. He was included. BENJAMIN STANTON. And now he was whooping with astonished triumph. BEST IN SCHOOL.

He'd done it. He'd come back from the brink. The T was missing and the JR, but that didn't matter. He knew who he was. And now, again, so would everyone else. BEST IN SCHOOL.

And everyone was flinging their arms around everyone else and shouting and cheering and whistling and Eddie seemed to be doing something like gargling. Ben abandoned himself to the celebrations. Kissed Cally: 'I knew you'd do it, Ben.' Kissed Lori: 'Well done, Ben. I'm really pleased for you.' Kissed Eddie: 'But, hey, Ben, no tongues, okay?'

'We've all passed, all of us.' Bex was still scouring the screen. 'The whole year group.'

'Yeah, so why's Macey looking so glum?' Jake nodded towards a crestfallen Simon Macey.

'Witnesses,' laughed Cally.

'What?'

'You'll see.'

They did. Later, after their euphoria had carried the students to the rec room.

'You're never gonna believe this,' someone hooted, darting in. 'Simon Macey's out there running around the quad. Naked!'

'What a horrible thought,' shuddered Bex. 'Someone ought to stop it.'

'Yeah, but not until we've all had a good laugh at his expense, right?' said Eddie. 'Come on, Bex. You can always cover your eyes.'

Less grudgingly than she appeared, Bex joined Eddie and most of the other students in the rush to witness Macey's humiliation. Ben remained where he was, leaning back in his chair and luxuriating in the moment. It was a great day to be alive. Particularly if you were Ben Stanton.

'Aren't you coming, Ben?' Cally had loitered behind.

'Nah. There'll be plenty of other chances to see Macey make a fool of himself. I like it just here right now.'

Cally glanced around. Only a scattering of students were still in the rec room, none within earshot. 'You'll be going to the ball tonight, though, won't you?'

'Try and stop me. Best in School doesn't miss occasions like that.'

A frown flickered across Cally's face but she continued

undeterred. 'Well, how about if . . . you and me . . . what if we, what I mean is . . .'

'You speaking in code, Cal?' Ah, the Stanton wit was flooding back.

'Would you like to take me to the ball? I'd like you to take me to the ball.' There. She'd said it.

'Well that's a very tempting offer, Cal,' conceded Ben grandly, 'and I'll certainly have a dance with you, but I think, tonight, there are gonna be plenty of people who'll want to dance with me, and I wouldn't want to disappoint my public.'

'I see.' Simon Macey wasn't the only one looking like an idiot right now.

'Yeah.' Ben made a cheery fist. 'The old Ben Stanton is back.'

'So he is,' Cally smiled thinly. 'I wish he wasn't.'

'Huh? *Cal?* What do you mean by that?' Ben called after her, but Cally was already in pursuit of her team-mates.

'Dad? It's me, Bex. Rebecca.'

She was standing in rooms to which no other student had access. Rooms that were private to the founder of the Deveraux College, the inspiration behind Spy High himself – Jonathan Deveraux. Bex's father. Bex's late father.

Jonathan Deveraux was now a computer program. His memories, his brain patterns, all preserved on microchips, his image made visible by pixels on a screen – on a circle of screens that descended from the ceiling. If he had blood, it coursed through the power that made the room hum and throb. If he had flesh, it was cold and metal, and it flickered with a million active circuits. If he had love, then it was part of the program.

'Can you hear me, Dad? Are you there?'

'I am always here.' The voice came from all around her, a perfect reproduction of the original, now issuing from an electronic larynx.

'I know that, Dad,' Bex said, 'but I'd like to see you.'

Her father's face appeared, grave, finely chiselled, hair greying at the temples, as it had been at his death a decade ago. 'I am here.'

'Thanks. It's good to see you.' Bex massaged the piercings in her ear as if they were giving her pain, as if they and the other outbreaks of metal in her skin were a rash that was itching. 'I wanted to tell you . . . though I guess you already know. I passed the exams. I graduated, Dad.'

Deveraux inclined his head in acknowledgement. 'Student Rebecca Deveraux,' he intoned. 'Highest mark, 87%. Lowest mark 54%. Aggregate mark, 70%. Pass.'

Bex's brow furrowed just a little. 'Yeah, I just wanted to let you know. Pretty good, huh? I mean, what with me starting late on the course and everything. Didn't think I'd make it once or twice.' She was feeding him lines. Tell me you're pleased, she was thinking. Tell me you're proud.

'You have done well, Rebecca,' said Jonathan Deveraux.

'You think so, Dad?' Bex brightened. 'I'm glad. I've really applied myself, you know? I didn't want to let you down, what with you getting the school up and started and —'

'Highest mark, 87%. Lowest mark, 54%. Aggregate mark, 70%. Pass.'

'Yeah.' Bex's head dropped. 'I passed.' Bitterly. 'Woohoo.'

Elsewhere, Jake was also experiencing a little parent problem, though in a rather different vein to Bex. At least Mr and Mrs Daly were both still alive. Unfortunately, they were also both still a long way from the Deveraux College – literally and metaphorically – sealed within one of the mid-west's vast agricultural domes, their horizons extending only as far as the great arches of steel and glass that protected the land inside from the ravages of pollution and terrorism.

They weren't coming to the graduation ceremony.

'What do you mean, you're not coming, Pa?' Jake was trying valiantly to keep his voice level, calm. His facial expression, a mixture of fury and frustration, was a more accurate guide to his emotions, but he could afford to look however he wanted. Domer farmers couldn't afford videphones. Jake was talking to his parents via the sound system only. 'You've got to come. You, Ma, Beth. It's my graduation.' He tried humour. 'You get to see me with a stupid flat hat on . . .'

'It's the farm, boy.' His father's voice, deadpan and distant, rendered even more remote by the poor quality of the Dalys' phone. 'We can't just go running off and leave the farm.'

'But the ceremony's not for a couple of weeks yet,' Jake pointed out. 'Can't you find somebody to look after the farm for a day or two by then?' He turned to Lori and shook his head in disbelief.

Lori looked on thoughtfully. How different Jake and his family were from Ben and the Stantons. Mr and Mrs S had probably already booked front row seats.

'Can't be done, Jake,' Mr Daly was claiming, not altogether unhappily, it seemed to her. 'There *is* no one. After the disaster, we're still trying to get things back to normal here. Everybody's got their own problems, don't need to share ours. And I don't have a son I can leave in charge . . .'

Ouch. Lori felt that one. She could see that Jake did, too. They both knew that in Mr Daly's ideal world, Jake would never have left the family farm in the first place. Bone of contention? More like a whole skeleton.

'Oh, thanks for that, Pa. Bit of a put me in my place there, yeah?' His voice was less level now, and not quite as calm.

'Just pointing out the reality of the situation,' claimed Mr Daly.

'Well, thanks for your support, Pa.' Jake's dark eyes blazed and the sarcasm in his tone was about to boil over into something worse, irreparable.

Lori squeezed his shoulder gently, and with her other hand covered the videphone's mouth-piece. 'Shouting at your Dad won't change his mind,' she whispered.

'But he can find someone. He's just doing this to punish me. I thought we'd resolved all that.'

'Jake? Are you still there?' crackled his father's voice. 'Liza, this blessed phone's playing up again!'

'End the call,' Lori advised, 'but do it *nicely*. Keep the invitation open. Tell your dad to phone back if the situation changes. We'll think of something. *I'll* think of something.'

'If you say so, Lori,' submitted Jake, 'but I'll be honest. I'm not going to hold my breath.'

Lori kissed her boyfriend lightly on the cheek. 'No problem,' she said. But inside, she wasn't so sure.

'You reckon you might let somebody else at the mirror any time before the party's over, Ben?' It was later that day. Eddie checked his watch. The music at the Finals Ball could already be playing. 'Or are you hoping it's gonna let you in on who's the fairest one of all?'

'I think it already has,' Ben said modestly. Stylishly short blond hair. Kind of hypnotic blue eyes. The square jaw and athletic body, nicely set off by the cut of his new jacket. And Best in School besides. Ben was gonna knock 'em dead tonight. He glanced across their room to Eddie's skinnier frame, the lank red hair and the clusters of freckles. Poor guy. It didn't help that he was in his underpants. 'Mirror's yours. Think you still need a bit of work.'

'Yeah, well, at least we haven't got to make space for Jake as well. He and Lori have already gone down, and a stunning couple they look too, if you don't mind me saying.'

'Why should I mind? Lori's nothing to do with me any more.' Maybe not, but when Ben had been imagining this evening in his head these past months, part of the plan had always been for him to enter the hall with Lori on his arm, the golden couple. Now he'd be entering with no one.

'That's a very mature attitude,' said Eddie, checking that his complexion was as zit-free as possible. 'You'll probably do all right tonight anyway. Sonia Dark'll be on the prowl – as always.'

'I think I can set my sights a little higher than Sonia Dark, thanks, Eddie,' huffed Ben.

'Oh, yeah, sure, I didn't mean anything.' For a guy who'd just been declared Best in School, Ben was touchy tonight. 'I mean, it's just not the same, though, is it?'

'Is *what*, Eddie?'

'Turning up at these gigs all brushed teeth and combed hair, maybe a few one-liners in the wings, hoping that some girl you haven't met yet is gonna like you. Instead of going with someone special. It's like waiting to be picked for the football team in sports lessons. You know, when I was younger I was always last. Even the fat kid and the kid with the glasses got picked before me.'

'It was obviously a traumatising experience for you, Eddie. Me, I was always the captain.'

'Well, we're in the same boat now, Cap.'

'Meaning?'

'Dateless for the dance,' Eddie sighed. 'In competition for somebody else's leftovers. Me, don't think I'll play. I'm gonna go round to the girls' room and tell Bex exactly how I feel about her, throw myself at her feet, kind of thing, though not exactly throw, you know. I mean, not literally splat on the floor. Yeah.' Eddie forced himself to stop. 'So what are you gonna do?'

And Ben suddenly knew precisely what he was going to do. He'd been stupid. He'd been blind. And he also suddenly knew what Cally had meant when she'd wished the old Ben Stanton away again. The arrogant Ben Stanton. The vain, selfish Ben Stanton. The Ben Stanton

who'd nearly ruined his chances at Spy High and condemned himself to mind-wipe.

The Ben Stanton who'd been admiring himself in the
mirror a few moments ago . . .

'Eddie, I love you.'

'Platonically, of course,' Eddie hoped.

'Give me five minutes. I need to go to see the girls
myself, but not Bex, don't worry. I need a word with
Cal.'

He was out of the room as if the fire alarm had just
gone off.

Eddie shook his head in bafflement. What was Ben
like?

Cally supposed she should have known better. The one
about leopards, spots and not changing them came to
mind as she slumped by her bed waiting for Bex to finish
her make-up. After all, hadn't it been Ben who'd wanted
her off the team in the early days, who'd ruthlessly
pushed for her to be removed? *Ping*. Correct answer. So
by what strange magic did she now expect him to have
been converted into someone who'd want to take *her* to
the Ball? As far as she could remember, Cinderella
hadn't had dreadlocks.

And why was she so cut up about it, anyway?

Because, during the Temple of the Transformation
affair, she'd seen a different Ben, more vulnerable,
more in need of help. Because he'd nearly lost everything he cared about but he hadn't given up, he'd
kept on striving. She could relate to that. She might
have been able to relate to Ben, if he'd given her the
chance.

'So what do you think?' Bex emerged from the bath-room fully made up.

Cally *thought* that Bex might have gained the same effect, and rather more quickly, had she simply thrust her head in a bucket of ink, but she *said:* 'Nice, Bex. Real distinctive.' There was a knock at the door. 'I'll get it.' Under her breath: 'We don't want to give whoever it is a heart attack.'

It was Ben. Cally caught her breath. Leopards. Spots. He tried to peer around her.

'Are you on your own?'

'No, Morticia Adams is with me.'

'I need to talk to you. In private.' He sounded like he meant it. 'Please, Cal.'

She didn't actually require much persuasion. 'Bex, I'm just talking to Ben. I'll be back in a minute.' She eyed him steadily. 'If not sooner.' Well, there was no need to let him think he'd have it all his own way.

He took her hand and led her a little way along the corridor to an alcoved window.

'All right, Ben, what do you want to talk about?'

'Me,' he said, which in itself was not unusual. 'And what an idiot I am. And how it was really bad the way I treated you earlier, after all you've done for me recently – following me to the Pleasure Mall, fighting the psimurai, helping me face finals. Unforgivable. But . . .'

'You hope I can forgive you anyway?'

'Can we replay the scene in the rec room? Only this time, I'll be you and you can be me and maybe this time, with any luck, it'll end differently. But it's up to you.' He cleared his throat dramatically. 'Would you like to come to the ball with me?'

A slow grin crept across Cally's face. 'I think I would. I'd like that.'

'So would I,' Ben said. 'Listen, Cal, no promises, no big declarations. Let's just have a good time together and see what happens.'

'I can hear the band playing now,' Cally said. 'I'll just pop back and tell Bex.'

'Don't worry about it.' Ben took her hand again. 'I don't think Eddie's going to want to be disturbed.' Cally looked quizzical. 'I'll tell you later. Come on. Cinders, you *shall* go to the Ball.'

When the next knock rapped on the girls' door, Bex assumed it was Cally. 'So what did Ben want, Cal?'

'I have no idea,' said Eddie, 'and people don't usually call me Cal.'

'Eddie. What do you want?' Which didn't sound encouraging. 'And what have you *got*?' Which sounded even worse.

Flowers in his right hand. Chocolates in his left. 'Didn't know which you'd prefer,' Eddie explained, 'so I brought both.'

'Why?' Bex seemed annoyed.

'Well, that's what boys do, isn't it, for girls they kind of feel strongly about. They bring them flowers. Or chocolates. I hope you like soft centres.'

'Eddie, I thought I'd made it clear.' Bex rolled the whites of her eyes in manacles of black make-up. 'I'm not interested in you that way.'

'And you'll probably need a vase of water for these before they wilt —'

'Hello! Eddie! Are you listening? I don't fancy you.

You don't turn me on. I don't want your hands on me. I don't want you cuddling up close to me. I don't want you thinking there's even a one in a million chance of you and me becoming an item. Are you clear? Do you want it in writing?'

'So . . . I guess coming to the ball with me's not really on, then?'

'Hooray! He finally gets the message.'

'Oh, yeah, he finally gets the message all right.' Eddie's brow furrowed uncharacteristically. 'But you can keep these anyway.' He unloaded his presents on Bex's bed. 'I've got no one else to give them to. I'll see you.' At the door. 'Hey, unless you see me first, right?'

Bex stared at the flowers and the chocolates for quite a while after Eddie's departure. Her expression was blank, like a mask. At last she picked the gifts up.

And deposited them in the bin.

The Finals Ball was different from the other discos and dances that were held at Spy High. No holograms of rock greats past and present. No modern technology at all. Just a real band playing real instruments. There was always a ready supply of musicians eager to sneak a peek inside the hallowed walls of the Deveraux College. It was just such a pity that, the next day, they could never remember anything about it to tell their friends. The school took no chances.

It had been a memorable ball tonight. Lori and Jake had maybe been the stars of the show, but the unexpected partnership of Ben and Cally had also made its mark on the dance floor – especially with Ben being surprisingly civil to Jake. And Lori had worried that his

Best in School award might have gone straight to his head.

Bex was all over the place, laughing loudly at odd moments and dancing with everyone. Only Eddie seemed out of sorts, stapled to a chair and staring glumly at the action as if an invisible barrier existed between him and it.

'Congratulations, Ben,' smiled Lori, who was sharing a slow dance with her ex-boyfriend for old time's sake. She'd judged it was safe and anyway, Jake was doing the same with Cally. 'You got what you wanted in the end, and in the end's all that matters.'

'Thanks, Lo.' He hadn't had her this near to him for a while. The memories still stirred. 'I expect you came a close second.'

Lori laughed. 'There's a Benjamin T Stanton compliment if I ever heard one. And what is it with you and Cally? Trading infiltration techniques?'

Ben glanced across to Cally. 'You'll know as soon as I know,' he mused. 'And as we seem to be into the intrusive observations, Lori, I see you're growing your hair longer again.'

'Well noticed.' She shook her blonde locks for emphasis and caught sight of Eddie. She frowned.

'What's bothering him tonight? He's usually the life and soul.'

'He was going to tell Bex how he felt about her,' Ben said. 'It sounded bad. And I don't think we need our training to work out her response.'

'That's terrible,' Lori said with sincerity. 'Eddie's nice. Bex could do worse.'

'She *is* doing worse. Look.'

Lori looked. Her heart sank. 'Oh, no.' Bex was getting up close and personal with none other than Simon Macey. Their mouths seemed glued together. 'Eddie is not going to like that.'

She was right. He didn't. He was already on his feet and heading towards them.

Several floors above the ball, in Jonathan Deveraux's rooms, the founder and Senior Tutor Elmore Grant were watching the Solartech plant burn.

'Forensics remain inconclusive, Grant,' said Deveraux, 'but terrorism or sabotage still remain the likeliest possibilities. Now that they have graduated, I want Bond Team fully assigned to an investigation of this matter. Call them for a preliminary briefing.'

'Now, sir?'

'Why not now, Grant?'

'It's eleven o'clock at night, sir.' Grant supposed he shouldn't be surprised at Deveraux's mystified reaction. Software didn't really have a concept of time.

'The enemies of tomorrow do not work to conventional timetables,' the founder observed.

'I appreciate that, sir,' conceded Grant, 'but it's the Finals Ball tonight as well. Do we really need to interrupt that? Can't the briefing wait until the morning?'

Deveraux considered. Sensors flickered in the ceiling, in the walls. The Senior Tutor ran his hands through his hair. 'First thing in the morning, Grant,' Deveraux decided. 'First thing.'

'Get off her! Leave her alone!' Eddie was piling into Simon Macey.

'Eddie, what do you think you're doing?' Bex was screaming in his ear.

'Nelligan, you nutter!' Simon Macey was flailing back at him.

'Ben,' said Lori.

'On it.'

Jake, too. Between them they grabbed Eddie's arms and hauled him off Simon Macey. 'Whoa, tiger,' Jake said.

'Hands off, Jake!' Eddie railed. 'This is none of your business. Did you see what he was doing to Bex?'

'With Bex!' Lori corrected. 'There's a difference. Oh, *Eddie*!'

'I ought to smash your face in,' Simon was saying.

'Don't push your luck, Macey,' Ben retorted.

The music had stopped.

Lori sighed. How come nothing ever went smoothly with Bond Team?

Whiteness. Endless and absolute. An environment with no discernible features to help judge distance or dimension. An empty world with only seven inhabitants, casting no shadow: Bond Team and Senior Tutor Elmore Grant.

It was the morning after the night before, and while the physical bodies of the new graduates were tucked up in their cyber-cradles back in the virtual reality chamber, their digitised consciousnesses were very much an active part of the program.

'Is everybody ready?' said Grant. 'All right then, let's start the briefing.'

Immediately the scene was transformed. A sky. Solid

ground. Before them, a factory or scientific installation of some kind. Lori read the sign: 'Solartech'.

'Exactly,' said Grant. 'Until a week or so ago, this was what the Solartech plant in Southern California looked like. It's a company specialising in solar power and its applications – solar fusion, solar reactors, things like that.'

'Wonder how long it took them to come up with the name,' joked Cally, before realising that she'd probably stolen Eddie's line. But from the look of him he didn't seem to care.

'Thank you, Cally,' the Senior Tutor acknowledged. 'As I say, that was the plant until very recently. Then this happened.'

Bond Team knew they couldn't be hurt. They knew the explosion wasn't real. But as Solartech fireballed and the flames engulfed them, they couldn't help but flinch.

'And we're suspecting foul play, right?' said Ben. 'I mean obviously. Secret agents don't deal with accidents, however terrible.'

'We suspect a deliberate attack, yes, though our playback program is still endeavouring to establish exactly how, and possibly who.'

'What's a playback program?' Eddie finally contributed. 'Sounds like a nostalgia show on TV.'

'Not quite,' said Grant. 'This is the playback program.' He indicated their surroundings. 'We're in it now. Initiate.'

And like film rewound, the flames rolled back, walls reformed, devastation reversed. It was a pleasant day in Southern California once more.

'If only we could bring back the people so easily,' said Lori.

'Follow me, please, Bond Team.' Grant led them towards the central building. 'What the playback program does is calculate and assess probabilities. The techs feed into it all the available information we have: the blueprints of Solartech, the names and histories of those people working in the plant at the time of its destruction, their duties, their routines. We've already been able to establish the origin of the explosion, so that intelligence, together with the blast's possible causes, is included as well. And putting all the data together, the computer constructs a model of the Solartech plant and how it might have been in the moments leading up to the disaster, determining the likeliest sequence of events in the hope that from the reconstruction we can learn something that we hadn't known before.'

'So we can relive the whole horrific thing as many times as we like?' Cally shuddered, even though the temperature in the program was precisely maintained. 'That's kind of sick, if you ask me.'

'Sadly,' Grant acknowledged, 'our work is not always pleasant.'

Bex watched a middle-aged man in a lab coat striding purposefully towards her. 'I'd keep going if I were you,' she advised him, 'but I guess it's already too late, poor . . . girl?' Within a single pace, the man had lost twenty years and changed sex, though *she* still kept the lab coat. 'Sir?' Bex addressed Senior Tutor Grant. 'What's *that* about?'

'Variables,' Grant illuminated. 'Recreating the past is not an exact science. We know roughly where Solartech's workers *should* have been and what they *should* have been doing, but as none of us were actually there, the computer can show us alternative scenarios, all of them within the realm of possibility. The first scientist you saw might have had business walking this corridor at this time, Bex, so that's one possibility, but so might the second.'

'Yeah, well one thing's guaranteed,' Eddie groaned. 'All these variables are giving me a headache.'

'Serves you right,' muttered Bex, loud enough for everyone to hear.

'I still don't quite follow,' Jake said. 'How can we use these options to pinpoint a culprit?'

'All right,' nodded Grant. 'Through here.' With the security guards ignoring them, Bond Team followed their Senior Tutor into a huge circular room where 'Danger' and 'Warning' signs were apparently breeding. Inside the room was another, equally circular but with no means of physical access. Only screens decorating the ultra-thick shielding revealed what was imprisoned within – a rotating sphere of fire, kept in place by powerful magnetic poles. Sensitive measuring instruments lining the shielding vibrated, as if shivering with fear. Perhaps they knew what was coming. 'A solar reactor,' introduced Grant, 'harnessing the almost limitless power of the sun, like an atom bomb without the mushroom cloud. An overload in the reactor here caused the explosion. Now, security is tight. It's almost impossible that anyone from the outside could have got in here undetected, and even if they did, only a very few highly specialised solar engineers would have had the know-how to effect an overload of the kind which evidently occurred. Therefore, firstly . . .'

'We're looking for someone inside the Solartech operation,' said Lori.

'And secondly . . .'

'He's got to be a top scientist, which narrows the field,' said Ben.

'Good. And in answer to Jake's question, that's why the playback program generates alternative scenarios.' Grant checked his watch before gesturing to the door. 'Because any one of these five people could be our saboteur.'

As if on cue, the door whisked open. A single scientist entered. He had five faces, each one battling for supremacy, like Dr Jekyll and Mr Hyde multiplied.

'Part of your mission, Bond Team,' said Grant, 'will be to discover which one.'

'But didn't you say there were no survivors, sir?' Cally asked.

'No *known* survivors. I'm afraid bodies are still being recovered and DNA tested.'

Eddie grimaced as the scientist switched from male to female to old to young. 'Now I've really got a headache.'

'But there's one aspect of this I don't understand,' Ben frowned. 'Why, sir? Even if our suspect somehow escaped, why would he do it? Why blow up the plant? Assuming he's not just working for techno-terrorists, who would gain from it?'

'An excellent question, Ben,' approved Senior Tutor Grant, 'and that's the other part of your mission. End playback program.'

They were in the white again, only this time they were not alone. Another man was with them, motionless and unblinking, a man of about forty, with oily, unhealthy skin, pale, watery eyes, and lips that were peeled back over slightly protruding teeth.

'Doesn't say much, does he?' said Eddie.

'Three-dimensional computer images usually don't, Ed,' tutted Cally.

'Bond Team,' said Grant, 'I'd like to introduce you to Mr Oliver Craven. You and he are about to get acquainted.'

TWO

Jake didn't even care about the mission. Here he was, out in the open with the nearest restricting dome hundreds of miles away, the sea wind in his face, flecks of salt on his lips as his AquaBike ploughed a foaming furrow across the water. And if that wasn't exhilarating enough, Lori was on the bike alongside him, blonde hair streaming. Jake laughed out loud. Life was good.

'What?' Lori called across.

'Nothing. Only, let's not go to Craven's party, Lo.'

'That's not a very secret agently attitude to take,' she grinned. 'And why not, might your team leader ask, Mr Daly?'

'It's too nice a day for espionage,' Jake declared. 'Let's just turn ourselves round, get back to shore, find a beach somewhere, chill out. Just you and me.'

'I think you need to keep your mind on the matter at hand, Jake,' grinned Lori, 'or Eddie and Cally really *will* feel aggrieved that I didn't give them this assignment.'

As the team's most skilful SkyBikers, Eddie and Cally had expected to be chosen for the little undercover escapade that Lori and Jake were now embarked upon. SkyBikes were not themselves involved, but transportation to Oliver Craven's estate was to be by AquaBike, their marine equivalent. Lori had pulled rank as team leader, however. She didn't foresee any danger that might necessitate the use of the AquaBike's weapons capabilities.

'And it might be wise,' she pointed out to Jake, 'to stop gawping at me and look where you're going.'

'What for? What am I gonna run into a mile from land?'

'That, maybe?' Lori pointed.

Jake followed her finger, whistled incredulously. 'I see what you mean, Lo.'

Ahead of them, looming massively on the horizon, was Oliver Craven's estate. Oliver Craven's *floating* estate. New Atlantis. It was as if tens of acres of land had simply been scooped up and deposited on the Atlantic ocean. Even from their limited vantage point so low to the water, Lori could see trees, and not just single trees strayed from the forest but a forest itself. She could see what looked like a French chateau on holiday from the Loire, its white stone walls and peaked turrets dazzling in the sun. And beneath the transported earth, she could see the structure's vast air cushions, protected by steel skirts, the apparatus without which Oliver Craven's pride and joy would sink helplessly into the depths. Lori had thought that some of the latest cruise ships were big, but New Atlantis reduced them to toy boats for a toddler's bath.

'Can you see this?' Lori marvelled, and not to Jake. 'Are you getting this?'

Back at Spy High, in Briefing Room One, her team-mates, Grant and Corporal Keene were gathered around a smart-screen. The screen was split down the middle. To the left the audience could see through Jake's eyes, to the right, through Lori's.

'The spy lenses are working perfectly, Lori,' said Grant. 'Just be careful with your eyes. Try not to rub them or anything. You too, Jake. They're still very sensitive.'

'Aren't we all?' muttered Eddie. He looked around the room again but no, just as before, one member of Bond Team was conspicuous by her absence. Bex.

'Will you look at that?' Ben was impressed. 'The technology that must have been required to build New Atlantis.'

'And the money,' commented Cally, 'money that could have been used to feed the starving, maybe.'

'Well,' mused Grant, 'money is one thing that Oliver Craven has plenty of.'

'Okay,' Lori was demanding of Jake, 'mind on the mission time. Recap. Oliver Craven. What do we know?'

'Not much.' Jake bade a mental farewell to visions of he and Lori on a beach. He and Lori aboard New Atlantis would have to do. 'Rags to riches cliché. Entirely unknown until about five years ago, then walks out of some nowhere town in Canada, shows some of his ideas for undersea exploration to the MD at Ocean Industries, gets taken on in Research and Development. Head of Research and Development within a year. Within another year the MD dies and he's Head of Ocean Industries. Over to you, Lo.'

'Okay,' Lori continued. 'Ocean Industries pursues an

aggressive takeover policy for companies engaged in similar work. It's renamed Craven Industries. Craven diversifies, patenting a range of technological advances but usually in the realm of taming and exploiting hostile environments. Becomes mega-rich. Not exactly reclusive, but very private. No girlfriends. No boyfriends. No family. No gossip. Just a name, a face, and a bank balance most countries would die for.'

'Yeah, and since the disaster he now owns Solartech as well, which *had* been resisting a takeover bid. That gives Craven a motive and us a reason for being here.'

'The anniversary of Oliver Craven's appointment to Ocean Industries,' said Lori. Music and laughter drifted to them on the breeze from New Atlantis. 'Sounds like the party's already swinging.'

Jake grunted. 'What are they playing? *"A life on the Ocean Waves"*?'

'Smile, Jake,' Lori reminded him. 'We're supposed to be excited.'

'I'm thrilled.' Jake checked his sleepshot wristbands. 'But I'm prepared.'

The Bond Teamers rounded the giant air cushions until they sighted New Atlantis's jetty, an appendage to the main structure where many vessels were already moored. Other guests, Lori noted, alerted by the distinctive whirr of rotorblades, were arriving by helicopter. There must be a heli-pad nearer to the chateau. Craven employees in smart nautical uniforms directed the AquaBikes to berths alongside the jetty, and helped to tie them up. Jake interpreted the bulges under their tunics as shoulder-holsters. Craven's men might have been smiling, but they too were prepared.

He wasn't surprised that their invitations were scrutinised closely. 'Jake Denver and Lori Archer, representing the Horizon Foundation for Under-Privileged Young People. Welcome. Please, follow me. Mr Craven would like to greet you.' The guy could have stared at the invite all day, though. A Spy High forgery was better than the real thing.

They were escorted up some steps to the higher levels of New Atlantis, well above its air cushions. Lori knew that, though at rest for the celebrations, the whole structure could sail at speeds of up to twenty knots, yet there was not the slightest sight nor sound of its engines. They were no doubt buried beneath deep soil. Indeed, if she hadn't had glimpses of the ocean all around, she'd have sworn they were on land.

Oliver Craven stood in a cordoned-off grove of trees beyond which impeccably clipped lawns extended past fountains and pools towards the chateau. There was polite applause as the music ebbed and flowed, the chink of crystal glasses. It was like any sophisticated garden party shoreside. Except maybe for the bodyguards in tuxedos on either side of Craven.

'The main man,' whispered Lori. 'So smile and *try* to look presentable.'

'I've changed my socks,' Jake grumbled. 'What do you want from me?'

Jake Denver and Lori Archer were introduced to Mr Oliver Craven. He seemed pleased to see them, offering his hand and opening his mouth a little wider. 'It's a pleasure to meet you both,' he said, in a voice that was a little too nasal to be impressive. 'The Horizon Foundation, yes. Do we support you? I suppose we must.' Lori Archer made charming and grateful mention of all the fine work that the foundation was able to do with under-privileged kids thanks to Mr Craven's generous contributions, but Mr Craven already appeared to have lost interest. Jake and Lori were invited to move along.

'Should have asked him if he'd had Solartech blown up, Ms Archer,' chuckled Jake. 'That might have kept his attention.'

'Well, with the formalities over we can get down to a bit of what we're here for,' said Lori.

'Sipping champagne?'

'Searching for secrets.'

'That's right,' said Senior Tutor Grant, watching his agents' progress. 'Head for the chateau. Work as a team. Keep an eye out for each other.'

Eddie leaned back in his chair and stretched dramatically, as if to suggest that he'd been cooped up too long. 'Well I hope they either find a hidden room or something or get jumped in the next five minutes, anything for a bit of action,' he complained. 'If this was a movie, it wouldn't get past the preview audience.'

'I'm sorry if you find real life espionage a little slow for your taste, Eddie,' said Grant wryly. 'Perhaps I'll ask Lori or Jake to risk their lives needlessly so you don't fall asleep on us.'

'No, sir. Sorry, sir,' Eddie grovelled. 'This is great. It's an education. Lori's technique, the way she praised Craven to his face, marvellous. But maybe just the occasional ninja . . .?'

Grant surveyed his students. 'Why hasn't Bex joined us yet? Cally, I thought you said she only had a slight headache and would be along shortly?'

'That's what Bex told me, sir,' Cally said. 'Maybe it's got worse.'

'She always has a headache when I'm around,' muttered Eddie.

Corporal Keene huffed scornfully. 'Headaches. A good secret agent can't afford to have headaches. Only thing that should keep a good secret agent from his work is having both his legs blown off, and even then . . .' Suddenly realising the import of his words, Keene turned abashedly to the Senior Tutor. 'Sorry, sir,' he said. Twenty years ago, that very eventuality had befallen Grant. His lower limbs now were entirely artificial.

'It doesn't matter, Corporal,' dismissed Grant. 'Your basic point is a good one. Cally, would you mind popping back to your room and informing Bex that we'd either like to see her here or in the infirmary at her earliest convenience.'

'Yes, sir,' said Cally. As she left the Briefing Room, the others returned their attention to the smart-screen.

Lori and Jake had entered the chateau. Most of the rooms looked like they still contained their original furnishings, all chandeliers and Louis XVI chairs. 'Craven can't *live* here,' Jake concluded. 'He might as well be pickled in aspic.'

'No help to us, either,' Lori agreed. 'This hallway along here, on the other hand . . .'

To Jake it appeared the same as any other of the halls they'd rambled through, nobody seeming concerned to stop them or ask them where they were going. Until he looked more closely. Then he saw that there was a clearly defined point beyond which the grain of the walls changed. 'A spot of interior decoration?' he pondered.

'Or a whole new extension,' Lori ventured. 'Whichever, I think this is the way to go.'

'Hey, you kids!' From nowhere, a Craven employee was bearing down on them. 'That's private through there. What do you think you're doing?'

Big, innocent smiles. 'We're looking for the bathrooms,' said Lori Archer.

'Yeah, well, they ain't that way. I'll show you, then I think you'd be better off rejoining the party.'

'Thank you. That's very helpful,' said Jake Denver.

'Sleepshot. Right between the eyes.' Jake Daly's view, as expressed a few minutes later, was not so friendly.

'Yes, that would have worked,' Lori observed sarcastically, 'if we'd wanted to get caught before finding anything out.'

They were in the gardens again. The party seemed to have moved on during their absence. The band had stopped playing and the guests were gathered around a sheltered podium on which stood Oliver Craven. He seemed to be in the middle of delivering a short, self-congratulatory speech. Jake and Lori added themselves to the fringe of the crowd.

'. . . all of you here have enjoyed some involvement with Craven Industries over the years. I am delighted that you have found the time to be with me today, to share this moment, not only to celebrate the past and our achievements thus far, but to anticipate successes yet to come.' Murmurs of assent from the assembly. 'Because let me assure you' – and here the speaker's teeth were unveiled in all their protruding glory – 'Oliver Craven has plans for the future the like of which none of you could ever imagine. I promise you that!'

Cheers. Applause. Cries of approbation.

A gunshot.

Sudden panic in the crowd. Women in fine dresses scattering. Rich men cowering. Craven employees running towards their boss, too slow. Jake and Lori tensed, alert, sleepshot poised to aim.

But nobody could stop the man with the gun from jumping on to the podium with a speed and agility belying his age. He had to be sixty or more. His stomach confirmed it, his balding head, his greying moustache, eyes that were old and almost dead. Maybe one more thing to see. His arm was round the startled Craven's throat, the gun at his head.

'Stay where you are! Stay where you are!' Directed at the security, no doubt, but obeyed by all. 'Anybody move, anybody *look* like they're going to move, and Oliver Craven is a dead man!'

Back in the Briefing Room, Eddie sat forward in his seat. 'Things are picking up at last.'

When Cally returned to the girls' room and found Bex evidently locked in the bathroom, she assumed that the headache had turned migraine and that her team-mate was engaged in the unpleasant task of heaving up most of the contents of her stomach.

Cally rapped on the bathroom door in what she hoped was a caring way. 'You okay in there? Bex?'

'Just a minute.'

Odd. Bex didn't sound weak or ill. And didn't look it, either, when she emerged in her bathrobe, with a towel wrapped round her hair as if she'd just been enjoying a long hot soak in the tub. 'Hi, Cal,' she said blithely.

'Bex?' Cally was puzzled. 'Are you okay?'

'Any reason why I shouldn't be?' Cally mentioned the apparent existence of a headache. 'Ah, no.' Bex winked conspiratorially. 'I made that up. Practising my disinformation techniques. Sorry.'

'So what have you been doing?'

'Oh. This and that.' Bex unwound the towel from her head. 'Particularly this.' Her hair was no longer purple but blue. 'Thought I needed a change. What do you think?'

'I think,' said Cally, 'that your priorities are as mixed up as your hair colour. Bex, Lori and Jake are on a mission right now, we're monitoring them in the Briefing Room, no simulations, no cyber-cradles, the real thing, and you lie to me so you can stay here and dye your hair?'

'Pretty much.' Bex turned towards her bed so that Cally couldn't see her face. 'And do you know how much like Ben you just sounded, Cal? You guys swapping lines now?'

'That's not funny,' Cally said. 'What's really going on, Bex?'

'I guess Eddie's in the Briefing Room, is he? Leaning back in his chair and making smart remarks every five minutes.' Bex snorted.

'We're all there,' Cally confirmed. 'Everyone but you.'

'Yeah, well I don't want to be where Eddie Nelligan is,' retorted Bex, flashing an angry expression at Cally. 'Not even in the Briefing Room. Not after the way he humiliated me the other night.'

'Actually, Bex, from where I was standing it looked more like you were humiliating Eddie.'

'Then you were standing in the wrong place.'

'Listen, what have you got against Eddie? Okay, so maybe he's not going to cut a second career as a male model, but none of us are exactly oil paintings, are we? Except maybe Lori. And Eddie's got other things going for him. He's amusing, he's fun to be with, he's loyal . . .'

'Sounds like a dog.'

Cally shook her head disapprovingly. She thought of Eddie risking his own life to save her during the Nemesis incident last year. 'He doesn't deserve to be treated the way you treat him, Bex.'

'Yeah?' Bex snapped. 'Well if Eddie's so wonderful, Cal, *you* go out with him.'

Cally pursed her lips thoughtfully. 'Words of advice, Bex,' she said. 'One, we've known Eddie longer than we've known you, so I wouldn't want you to be thinking about that whole taking sides thing. Two, you should probably get some clothes on and join the rest of us right now. If Grant finds out you've been pulling a fast one I doubt even your dad'll be able to help you.'

Bex watched Cally leave sullenly. What gave her the right to dispense words of advice like a doctor prescribing pills? But she reached for her ShockSuit anyway, because, unpalatable as it was, Cally was certainly right about one thing. These days, she'd be foolish to rely on her father for anything.

'What do we do?' Lori hissed, to Jake, to Grant, to anyone. Though there were plenty of Craven's men now encircling the podium, none dared shoot for fear of hitting their employer and almost certainly blighting their pension prospects. 'We could use our sleepshot, but then we'd blow our cover.'

'Down to you, Lo. This is team leader stuff.'

'Jake's right,' Grant's voice confirmed in her earpiece. 'The decision is yours, Lori. Risk a possible fatality or risk the mission.'

It was like being on a game show, Lori thought, only instead of cash and consumer durables, for a secret agent the stakes were life and death. 'We wait,' she determined, and hoped she sounded positive.

'It's all right! It's all right!' the man with the gun was shouting from the podium. 'I don't want to hurt any of you.' Most of the assembly didn't appear entirely convinced. 'There's only one man here I want to hurt. But you're all my witnesses. I need you to hear some things first.' The man's brow wrinkled as if in pain. 'You may not know who I am, but your generous, charitable host Mr Oliver Craven does, don't you, Craven? Don't you?' The proximity of gun to forehead seemed designed to prompt Oliver Craven's memory. 'Tell them!'

'Sir?' asked Lori. Back in the Briefing Room, the elderly man's image was being fed into the recognition computer.

'He's Douglas Neil Elleray,' Grant transmitted.

From the podium, Craven confirmed the fact.

'And what do I do?' Elleray pursued. 'What *did* I do?'

Grant and Craven this time spoke in unison. Douglas Neil Elleray was the Head of Solartech. *Had* been Head of Solartech. Very much past tense.

Very much motive for murder, Lori thought.

'You took it away from me,' the old man was wailing. 'You *stole* it from me. Everything I'd worked for, everything that made my life mean anything, it's all gone. And you're responsible, Craven.' Bitterness merged into anger. Self-pity into rage.

'Lo, he's going to do it,' Jake judged. 'Psychological profiling. Desperate men do desperate things. He's got nothing to lose. His self-control's disintegrating. He'll kill Craven. We can't wait —'

'We have to wait.' Lori was adamant, surprising herself. She was thinking of the Solartech disaster. She was thinking of the mission.

'You did it, didn't you?' Elleray was accusing. 'I know you did. I want you to tell all these fine people gathered here to sing your praises the truth, Craven. The *truth*!'

'I have no idea what you're talking about, Douglas,' Craven attempted to soothe, 'but if you calm down I'll get my doctors to have a look at you and I'm sure we can work something out. Business is business, Douglas.'

'Business?' Elleray was shaking as if he might explode. 'You destroyed my plant. You murdered all those people, innocent people. All because I wouldn't sell. It was my life's work, I couldn't sell my life's work.'

'You're ranting, Douglas,' observed Oliver Craven. 'Please calm down.'

'I wanted you to know,' Elleray addressed the crowd. 'I wanted you to know what kind of cold-blooded killer you've all come here to celebrate. Whatever lies he spreads, I'm telling you all, Oliver Craven caused the Solartech catastrophe. He probably murdered Clem Mackintosh at Ocean Industries as well to become MD. This is the man you've been applauding. He's a monster, a monster. And I . . .' Elleray suddenly seemed to lose his thread. He gazed about him as if awaking in an unknown place. He was a broken old man with a gun, a gun that now seemed heavy in his hand. His arm dropped to his side.

'Good choice, Lo,' whispered Jake.

Craven was wresting himself free from the old man's grasp.

'I just wanted to tell . . . somebody . . .' Years heaped on Elleray's head. And then he vanished from view as Craven's men closed in around him.

The guests pressed forward too, now that there seemed little danger of concluding their party in Casualty. At least, most of the guests did.

'Come on,' Lori urged her partner. 'While everyone's occupied with Elleray. It's time for searching the chateau: take two.'

This time, nobody appeared to prevent further exploration of the newly added corridor, but Lori knew that a successful team leader – one who tended to survive her missions – didn't take chances.

'You'd better stay here, Jake. Keep watch. Make excuses if anybody comes.'

'You sure it isn't safer if we keep together?' It wasn't that Jake resented taking orders from a girl, least of all Lori, but guard duty simply wasn't his style.

'Grant'll use your lenses to let me know what's happening,' Lori said. 'Just don't shut your eyes. I'll be quick, promise.' She kissed him on the cheek.

'I'll be waiting. Promise that, too.'

Lori darted deeper into the chateau, swiftly and silently. She'd believed what Douglas Elleray had said, regardless of his obviously unbalanced state of mind. She sensed that Oliver Craven was capable of slaughtering all those people in order to get what he wanted – there was something about him, something kind of sinister – but belief was never good enough. There had to be proof. Elleray clearly didn't have it, but maybe it was hiding in these corridors, just waiting for someone to come along and find it.

She went through one room after another. There was no more antique furniture, just offices. Offices that seemed above board and innocent. Nobody was at work, no doubt because of the party, but they'd tidied up behind them. The computers were all switched off. Lori calculated that it wasn't worth her while hacking into any of them. She doubted that Craven would trust any incriminating files to a computer in general use.

Then she came to a locked door, the first to be so secured. Locked doors usually meant something impor-tant on the other side. Lori selected the deactivator from its capsule on her belt and placed it over the lock mech-anism. Within three seconds, the door was no longer a barrier to her investigations.

'Could be it,' she breathed. A study. Rich leathers and mahogany. Likely to be the domain of one man only. Lori eased the door closed behind her. She had an idea she wouldn't want to be disturbed for the next few minutes.

Though traditional in style, the desk was a smart-desk, the inlaid computer screen operated by a keyboard. Lori set about bypassing its security program. 'Is Cal there?' she grinned. 'Ask her how I'm doing.'

'Just fine.' Cally's voice. 'You'll soon be catching me up as Bond Team's hacker supreme, Lo. Just be a little careful here. Try . . . That's it. You're in.'

Oliver Craven's private files. Already, courtesy of her

spy lenses, everything that Lori could see was being transferred back to Spy High and assimilated by the Deveraux computers. She didn't need to read it herself. All she needed to do was to keep clicking through the files and Craven's secrets would be forced to reveal themselves. At least, that was the plan. Some of the files, she noticed, appeared to be in code.

'Lori,' Grant interrupted in a voice that suggested her time might well be up, 'Jake's got company. Two men. One's escorting Jake outside, and if he can just turn his head . . . Yes, the other's heading your way. Unlikely he's got access to Craven's study, but even so . . .'

'Out of here,' Lori consented, closing the files and deactivating the smart-desk. She moved with smooth efficiency to the door. Agents in the field should never rush. Haste led to panic, and panic led to mistakes. Mistakes were bad. Very much in control of herself, Lori placed her fingers on the door handle.

She let out a cry and that was bad too but there were extenuating circumstances. Suddenly dropping into a circular chute like the insides of a steel snake was not an everyday occurrence, even for a graduate of Spy High. Lori tried to slow her frantic descent but there was nothing for her to hold on to. Wherever she was heading, she was going to get there quickly. 'Sir!' She tried to raise Grant. As her body collided with the sides of the chute, his voice could only crackle incomprehensibly in what Lori realised with growing anxiety was a great deal of distance. Her head cracked against metal. Beneath her, unavoidable, inevitable, were dark waters like the bottom of a well. Lori had time for a single deep breath.

Before she plunged right into them.

And half the screens in Briefing Room One went blank.

'Lori . . .' Ben gasped.

'She'll be fine.' Senior Tutor Grant eclipsed further expressions of concern. 'Her fall's damaged the spy lenses, that's all.'

'That's all?' Ben wasn't satisfied. 'We've got to do something.'

'There's nothing *we* can do,' Grant pointed out. 'Lori's trained, like all of you. She's team leader. She'll find a way to survive.'

Which was pretty much the thought going through Lori's mind at the same moment. The shock of sudden and total immersion in the icy water of the ocean beneath New Atlantis was wearing off. Now she had to think and now she had to act. She must have missed a safety code on the smart-desk or something, triggered a trap. But right now that was the least of her concerns. She had to worry about breathing.

She reached for an item on her belt, feeling reassured as she fitted it into her mouth. A belt-breather, like a boxer's gum-shield but allowing its wearer some ten minutes of air supply, more than sufficient time to reach the surface. She hoped.

There was no trace of light above her, only a greater looming darkness, the underside of New Atlantis. The chute had evidently sealed itself to prevent any luckless victim from trying to climb back up, even if that were possible. No problem. All Lori had to do was thrust out away from the body of Craven's estate and then rise to the world of light and air again. Not much of a death trap, really, when you thought about it. Wouldn't even make the Stromfeld program.

Lori swam. She managed five strokes before she struck something invisible and unyielding. Some kind of barrier, it seemed, maybe plexi-glass, and slightly concave too, as Lori felt with her fingers. So that was how Craven meant to eliminate even those of his enemies with strong swimming strokes and powerful lungs. Lori was in a tank and there was unlikely to be an exit.

She pressed a stud in the centre of her belt. Time to shed a little more light on the situation. A yellow beam stabbed through the water. Lori widened its range, allowing her to view her immediate environment more clearly for the first time. Maybe not such a good idea.

It seemed she wasn't alone in the tank after all. Something else was in there with her. Something that seemed interested to see her.

A shark.

THREE

'Jake, move it!' Ben's voice hammered in his ear. 'Every second could be vital!'

'What, you think I'm gonna stop and sight-see on the way?' Jake hurtled across the pristine lawns of New Atlantis. Where did Stanton get off adding his commands to Grant's? He wasn't team leader any more. And what, did he think *he* cared more for Lori? Well, Jake was going to prove him wrong.

He raced through the woods, startling guests who were beginning to drift towards their own transport. The sun was dipping low to the far horizon.

Grant again: 'Take the bikes to the chateau side, Jake. Dive there.'

'Yes, sir.' Obviously. Did they think he was stupid?

At the steps to the jetty a Craven employee interrupted his polite chit-chat with departing guests to frown suspiciously at the boy charging recklessly towards him. He'd had one too many surprises already this afternoon, and put out his arm to pause Jake. 'Hold on a second, laddie . . .' But every second counted. Jake took the offer of the arm, wrenched and threw the man with perfect skill.

'Sorry. Can't wait.' Took the steps three at a time. If he slipped, he'd fall and break his neck. He didn't slip.

'Stop him! Stop that kid!' The man he'd upended was yelling for reinforcements. A colleague on the jetty was blocking Jake's path. He lunged. Jake dodged, swept with a powerful leg. And a second Craven employee was off his back.

Jake jumped into the saddle of his AquaBike. There was no time to untie it from its mooring. He released his belt-blade and slashed at the restricting ropes, did the same for Lori's machine.

Craven's men were pounding down the jetty towards him.

But it would make no difference. Jake thrust his AquaBike into reverse, at the same time activating the remote signal so that Lori's would follow his every move even without a rider.

With a sudden shoot of spray that lashed across the jetty and drenched his hapless pursuers, Jake arced the bike around and stamped on the accelerator. He didn't look back.

Lori needed him.

The perfect eating machine, she'd seen a programme about it. All a shark did was devour, digest and defecate, and it wasn't particularly fussy about its prey. Lori recalled a boy once telling her that she looked good enough to eat. Seemed he was right.

The shark was zeroing in on her, a torpedo of muscle and sinew and hacksaw teeth. Her back was against the wall, literally, her mind reeling, the instinct to panic pumping hotly in her heart. She had to remember who she was, focus on her training, on her skills.

The creature's eyes stared, pitiless.

Do something.

Its mouth a yawning black maw.

Sleepshot.

She raised her arm to fire but her movements were slowed by the water. The shark was almost upon her, grinning with hunger in the yellow splash of her belt-beam. Shrinking back, her feet braced against the barrier. She pushed. She powered. She propelled herself forward. Too late for the shark to change its course. It rammed into the plexi-glass as Lori swam with desperate strength to put distance between her and the predator. There was no fooling herself, though. In this tank she could not escape. She had to eliminate the shark.

It twisted sinuously in the water to attack again, moving with a fluid grace at odds with its deadly, glittering jaws and baleful eyes. The collision had not improved the creature's mood.

But this time Lori was ready. She'd turned, arms outstretched as she trod water and fought to keep balanced, and fired from both wrists, the projectiles hissing through the deep, embedding themselves in the shark's vulnerable flesh. She couldn't miss and she didn't stop.

Neither did the shark. Unbelievably, it kept on coming. Lori kept on firing because there wasn't anything else for her to do and if the sleepshot didn't take effect within the next five seconds it wouldn't make any difference anyway, because by then the creature's bear-trap teeth would have made stumps of her arms.

Lori thought of Jake. She thought of Ben. She thought of closing her eyes.

The shark rolled, writhed, thrashed in the water. It seemed suddenly heavy, not lithe. Its trajectory dipped. Its mouth drooped. A dead weight, it drifted towards the bottom of the tank.

Lori didn't bother wishing the creature sweet dreams. She had no idea how long the effect of the sleepshot might last, and she wanted herself permanently removed from the menu before the shark recovered.

She swam back to the barrier. There was only one way of penetrating that – the nitro-nail she'd thought to tape to the index finger of her left hand was the afternoon's sole stroke of luck so far. She tore it off quickly and pressed it against the plexi-glass. Lori hoped it would be powerful enough to break through. If not, she had about five minutes to compose her own obituary.

Underwater, the sound of the nitro-nail exploding was muffled. Its force, though, was no less effective than on land. An exit as jagged as the shark's teeth opened for Bond Team's leader.

And she needed it. She was through in an instant, striving out and up for the surface. Her encounter with the shark, the adrenaline that it had quickened through her veins, had increased consumption of her belt-breather's air supply. Her lungs were beginning to contract, to wring out their remaining traces of oxygen. She had a useless lump of metal in her mouth. There was pressure on her chest. And minutes had suddenly shrunk to seconds.

Lori hauled herself upwards with ragged strokes, a climber scaling an impossible cliff.

Think air. Believe in breath. If this was going to be the final one, make it last. She felt her eyes glazing. She felt herself drowning. Sheer willpower kept her muscles working.

Before her eyes, lights danced, glistening flecks of white, like a ceiling studded with jewels. Then Lori shattered the surface like glass, gulped the air in deep, sweet draughts. She was laughing, whooping. She plucked the belt-breather from her mouth and cast it aside. What Grant had once said was true. You only fully appreciate life when you've stood on the brink of death.

'Lori! Lori!' Jake was speeding towards her, New Atlantis towering a little distance beyond. She didn't plan on going back *there* in a hurry, at least not without a swimsuit. 'She looks okay, can you see?' Jake reported eagerly back to Spy High. 'I think she's okay.'

'I will be,' Lori called, 'soon as I get back on to dry land.'

Jake drew up the AquaBikes alongside his girl-friend. 'Don't worry,' he said. 'The party's over. But I think we kind of outstayed our welcome.' He helped her out of the sea and onto her bike. 'We'll be shoreside in no time. But just to keep you going . . .' He pressed his lips to hers and didn't care that she was getting him soaking wet.

'Douglas, Douglas, Douglas, what are we to do with you?' Oliver Craven tutted like a weary headmaster with a repeatedly recalcitrant pupil. He was pacing a room in the chateau that also had elements of school about it: desk, chairs, bookcases. But it would have been an unusual school indeed to permit its students to be bound and gagged as tightly as the struggling figure of Douglas Elleray. Craven leaned closer to the older man, shook his head sadly. 'Interrupting my speech like that, wielding a firearm.' The one Craven now weighed in his hand. 'So impolite. And don't you know these things can be dangerous, Douglas? You might have hurt yourself.' He lifted the gun to Elleray's shining pink forehead. 'Of course, you still might.'

Elleray's eyes widened in terror. Indecipherable sounds emerged from behind the gag.

Craven chuckled and placed the gun on the desk. 'But nobody here wants to hurt you, Douglas. We want to help you.' He patted his prisoner's cheek. 'You're obviously a little upset about losing Solartech and feel you need to lash out. That's understandable. You've lost everything. I'm sympathetic, believe me, but we'll take good care of your work – the Prometheus Project in particular, as you can imagine. And Douglas, it wasn't I who destroyed your plant, and just to prove that there are no hard feelings, I'm going to tell you who it was.' He activated the communicator on the desk. 'You can come in now.'

Elleray snapped his attention to the door. It opened. Three men came in. Two of them were Craven's employees and he didn't recognise them. The third was not and he did.

'Dr Charles Bain,' said Oliver Craven of a thin, apologetic man with eyes that didn't seem able to open properly. 'I'm afraid it seems that my pay and conditions are rather more attractive than yours. The bonus for temporarily overloading a solar reactor, apparently, is particularly generous.'

'Sorry, Mr Elleray,' shrugged Dr Charles Bain, 'but I needed the money.'

Craven listened to the gagged man's ravings as if he understood them. 'Hmm,' he mused. 'I don't think you can expect a reference, Bain.' He clapped his damp hands, became business-like and brisk. 'Well, it's been pleasant, Douglas, but one of us still has a company to run. Time for you to go.' The two employees bore down on Elleray. 'But don't worry, we know you're not well. Everyone who saw you this afternoon knows you're not well. So we're going to take you to a hospital.' Elleray was hauled to his feet and dragged towards the door. Behind the gag, he seemed to be howling. 'No, really, Douglas, there's no need to thank me.' To the nearest lackey, in an undertone: 'Please, take bad care of him.'

Bain was about to follow the others out but Craven called him back. 'Yes, sir?'

'Loose ends, Bain.'

'I beg your pardon, sir?'

'Are you aware that Elleray's melodramatic little outburst was not the only compromise of security New Atlantis suffered this afternoon?' Bain admitted warily that he'd heard rumours. 'An intruder masquerading as one of my guests – and representing a charity, too! What is the world coming to? – broke into my study and rifled through some of my files. A girl, and a teenage girl at that. Why she isn't making out with some pimply youth in the back seat of a wheelless instead of engaging in espionage activity I simply fail to understand.'

'I don't,' Bain blurted, 'I don't know anything, sir.'

'Of course you don't.' Craven sounded offended. 'I'm not accusing you, Bain. I'm explaining my reasons.'

'Reasons, sir?' The engineer did not appear entirely relieved.

'Loose ends, and why, if some shadowy government organisation is finally turning its bleary eyes upon us, why we need them to be tied up.'

Bain nodded. 'To protect ourselves. To protect the plan.'

'I'm glad you're so understanding. That makes it so much easier for me.'

'Sir?'

Craven picked up the gun from the desk. 'Elleray had two shots left,' he observed. 'Seems a pity to waste them.'

The reporter on the view-screen wasn't holding out much hope. 'Though the wreckage of the helicopter has been located,' she supplied, 'divers are still searching for any sign of the pilot or of Mr Elleray himself. There seems little chance that the industrialist and pioneer of solar engineering will be found alive. Having apparently suffered a minor nervous breakdown while aboard business rival Oliver Craven's magnificent floating estate New Atlantis, Douglas Elleray was being flown to the Lord Have Mercy Hospital in Florida when the accident occurred . . .'

'Accident,' sniffed Jake, as Senior Tutor Grant asked the smart-desk to end playback there. The news report obediently froze and vanished.

'Indeed,' agreed Grant. He scanned every member of Bond Team as they sat attentively around the table in

Briefing Room One. Even Bex had been prompt to this meeting, with no hint of a headache. 'And as we know now that his body has been recovered, Elleray was killed in the helicopter crash.'

'And no trace of the pilot.' Bex was obviously keen to prove her presence. 'I mean, is that a giveaway or what? Why aren't the cops knocking at Craven's door already?'

'Possibly because the police, Bex,' suggested Grant, 'do not have access to quite the same information as ourselves.'

'Yeah,' piped up Eddie. 'Thanks to our noble leader doing her audition thing for "Jaws 12".'

Lori smiled and shuddered at the same time. It didn't do to dwell on narrow escapes. She felt Jake's fingers finding hers.

'Yes,' acknowledged Grant. 'Well, many of the files Lori was able to gather for us were of a routine nature, as might have been expected, but many were also of interest. The most intriguing of all seem to be written in some kind of code that we've so far been unable to crack. Our best cryptographers are working on it now. Fortunately, a number of these include a diagrammatical element, and that we *can* translate. For example. Desk: display Craven file ZX9.'

A series of blueprints appeared on the smart-desk's screen. The notation on them was a jumble of impenetrable symbols, but visually they seemed to represent the outline and electrical innards of a mechanical device shaped somewhat like a spread-eagled octopus with tentacles tapering into drills.

'Anybody care to tell us what it is?' Grant offered.

'Sure,' said Eddie. 'What about giving us the first letter?'

'First letter is bang, Ed,' said Ben. 'That's a bomb. And a big one. We're not talking minor, blow a door off its hinges explosions with this baby.'

'And look at all that cabling,' Cally noted, narrowing her eyes thoughtfully, 'all connected to the main device. And the drills. For burrowing into the ground?'

'Or the sea bed,' said Grant. 'The only words on these prints in English seem to be place names, and one in particular. Honolulu. Craven Industries has holdings in Honolulu.'

'Tell me that's Honolulu, Hawaii and not Honolulu, Idaho,' Eddie begged.

'Hawaii, of course,' sighed Grant, 'which means that some of you need to fly down there and find out what, if anything, is going on.'

'Aloha!' Eddie was already on his way. 'I love this job!'

'*Some* of us?' Lori prompted.

'That's right. There's something else that's come to our attention.' Grant addressed the furniture. 'Desk. Display Dr Charles Bain.'

'Who's he?' Bex wanted to know as a thin apologetic man appeared on screen. 'And what's the matter with his eyes?'

'Squinting at the sun too long,' said Jake. 'He's one of the five, isn't he, sir? From the playback program. One of the solar engineers at Solartech. One of the guys who could have done it.'

'Good, Jake,' nodded Grant, 'and the *only* member of the entire facility still unaccounted for. Which rather suggests he was not present at the time of the actual explosion. So it might be worth our while trying to find him.'

'Can we hope he's fled to somewhere exotic too?' Cally ventured.

'And finally,' Grant continued, ignoring her, 'Mr Deveraux feels it would be useful to explore further into Oliver Craven's background, to fill in the blanks, as it were. So a third team will go to Littleport, Nova Scotia.'

'Nova where?' Eddie was aghast. 'Don't you have to have a beard and wear galoshes to go there? Think I'll stick with Hawaii, if that's okay with you, sir.'

'Well,' the Senior Tutor was raising his hands and shaking his head, 'the allocation of team resources now that you've graduated is no longer my immediate responsibility. Three missions, three teams. That's my contribution. Exactly who goes where, that's why we have team leaders. Lori, it's over to you.'

From a Spy High point of view, it was a pity that Lori's investigation of Oliver Craven's private study had been so rushed. Had she found more time to look around, she might have noticed the circular mirror set into the wall, and then, almost certainly for somebody with her observational skills, she would have registered that the glass did not actually show a reflection, and it would have occurred to her that a mirror that did not show a reflection was a mirror doomed to fail in its primary function. Unless, of course, its primary function was not that of a mirror at all.

Oliver Craven stood before it now, and the face at which he glanced but dared not stare was not his own.

'Security at all our locations has been increased as you instructed,' Craven reported, more like a lackey himself now than the Managing Director of a vast multi-national. 'There have been no further incidents.'

'So far.' The cautioning voice from the mirror-screen was harsh, grating, somehow foreign. 'But until we know who this girl and boy are, we cannot be certain that there will continue to be none.'

'No. No.' Craven hung his head. 'I suppose not.'

'We will therefore move to the final phase immediately. Now that we have control of Solartech's Prometheus Project, there is no need for delay in any case. Transfer personnel and equipment to the Fortress accordingly. Then you must make a last visit to our Molohalu operation. You understand what needs to be done?'

'Of course.'

'Good. Then do it. The moment of our triumph is all but upon us.'

There was a puzzle that had fascinated Lori as a child. It had once belonged to her grandmother, and partly she'd loved it because of that and partly because it had seemed so old and unfashionable, no need to plug it in or boot it up or anything. It was just fifteen small plastic lozenges slotted into a square of similar material that had enough space for sixteen. The lozenges were initially positioned at random, but each one bore part of a picture on its surface, and if you moved them around correctly, one slot at a time, precisely, painstakingly, eventually the chaotic individual little pieces would come together to form a single harmonious whole – the big picture. The puzzle, Lori remembered, had kept her busy for hours.

Working out the pairings of Bond Team wasn't far behind.

She and Jake, of course, but as they'd already enjoyed the hospitality of New Atlantis, Lori thought something more sedate might be appropriate. They'd head north to Littleport. As for the others, she'd originally assumed Ben and Cally/Bex and Eddie, but given the recent friction between the latter, she doubted that was a good idea. So Ben and Eddie/Bex and Cally? Single-sex teams weren't usually encouraged at Spy High, one reason why the gender balance in each major team, and in the school as a whole, was maintained strictly fifty-fifty. Males and females brought with them different strengths, different weaknesses. Individually, they were part of the picture. Only together, complementing each other, were they the whole.

So that left Ben and Bex/Eddie and Cally. Ben might not like it. He and Cally seemed to be getting close. But he had worked well with Bex before, and Lori figured there was always the argument of absence making the heart grow fonder. Besides, a Cally/Eddie partnership would bring the team's two top SkyBikers together, and with AquaBikes operating on pretty much the same principles, that made Lori's decision as to mission selection all the easier. Even if Ben was annoyed, Eddie would be pleased with her.

'Yo Waikiki, here we come!'

Lori was right. And it was impressively done, because throughout his extended celebrations, Eddie managed to glance at Bex not even once.

'So I get to track down Dr Charles Bain.' Right again.
'With Bex.' Any less enamoured and Ben might have
tripped over his lower lip.

'So what are we waiting for?' Eddie was grinning.
'When's our flight? Cal, you reckon we've got time to
buy surfboards? They'll help us blend right on in.'

'Wait,' Lori called. 'Eddie, can you wait? Whatever
you're hoping, this isn't a vacation, for you, for any of us.
We already know what can happen on missions. We
know the dangers.' She thought of Jennifer. At times like
this, she was still with them. 'But we've come through so
far and mostly we've faced them together.' She thought
of the puzzle again, the splintered segments meaning
little. 'But this time, for now at least, we've got to split
up. It might be a while before we see each other again.
And our first real graduate operation. I don't know —'
Lori seemed suddenly aware that everyone else was
gazing at her — 'I just thought, before we go, we ought to
all wish each other luck.'

'Sure,' supported Jake. 'Goes without saying, Lo.
Luck, Eddie. Don't get sunburn.'

'Take care, Cal.' Ben hugged her, didn't really want to
let her go.

'You, too.' The feeling seemed mutual.

'I'll see you soon.'

'You bet, Mr Best in School.'

And Bex had been avoiding it, but at last there was
only Eddie left to embrace. An uncomfortable handshake substituted. 'Don't do anything stupid,' she said
awkwardly.

'Stupid?' A sly smile. 'This is Eddie Nelligan you're
talking to.'

'I know. That's what I'm afraid of.'

'Don't worry about me, Bex.' With a farewell salute. 'You never have done before.'

Lori looked around at her team-mates, Jake by her side. 'Now I guess we *had* better go,' she said. And be safe, she was thinking. Whatever lay ahead, be safe.

FOUR

Their plane touched down in Honolulu on the island of
Oahu almost exactly on time. Eddie and Cally col-
lected their bags from the appropriate carousel, had their
retinas scanned along with their fellow passengers, and
made their way towards Arrivals.

'Don't have to put your shades on yet, Cal,' Eddie
commented as a pair of stylish sunglasses made an
appearance. 'We're still in the terminal.'

'Oh, it's not the sun I'm worried about,' said Cally. 'It's
the possible long-term effects on my vision of your shirt.
It ought to come with a health warning.'

'It is rather special, isn't it?' Eddie congratulated
himself, gazing down admiringly at the dazzlingly
bright creation he was wearing. 'Radiation yellow, they
call it.'

'I bet they do. Listen, Eddie – ' pausing as if she wasn't
quite sure how to phrase her next words – 'you don't
have to try too hard, you know?'

'Try too hard to what?'

'To make out you're not still upset about Bex. To pretend she doesn't matter.'

Eddie's trademark grin twitched but didn't falter. 'Bex, yeah. I wonder what her hair would look like in radiation yellow. Kind of glowing, I reckon.'

'Eddie, I know you're hurt. Anyone would be.'

'Hurt?' Eddie tried a dismissive grunt. It wasn't convincing. 'Do I look like I need a doctor? No, Cally, thanks for caring and all that kind of stuff, but I'm fine. This shirt and my mood, same thing. I just know where I stand, that's all. So I might not have hooked Bex but there are plenty more fish in the sea, and Hawaii's just *surrounded* by ocean.'

'If you say so, Eddie,' said Cally sceptically. 'Just try not to drown, okay?'

By now they'd reached the main terminal building. Around them people milled holding pieces of card with names written on them, eager relatives waiting for loved ones, holiday reps with plastic smiles, bored drivers with no smiles at all.

'I don't see a Nelligan or a Cross,' observed Eddie.

'No sweat. He'll be here.' The Bond Teamers were to be met at the airport by Spy High's Selector Agent in Hawaii, a man named Ken Ho.

'I tell you what I do see, though,' Eddie nudged. A Polynesian girl not far away, a girl their own age, thick black hair and stunning in a simple floral dress. 'Vid Ken and tell him to take his time.'

Cally saw the girl, too. She sighed exasperatedly. 'Heel, hormones, heel.'

'She's looking at me, Cal. She's looking at me.' As indeed seemed to be the case. And she was smiling, too.

Sometimes even Eddie's delusions could have foundation in fact. 'It's the shirt. I knew it. Listen, you wait here for Ken Who . . .'

'Ho.'

'Whatever. I'll be right back. See the way she's smi—'

But as Eddie took his first step towards her, the black-haired girl turned. She didn't just walk away, either. She *ran*.

'What?' Eddie's grin crumbled like a sandcastle in the surf. 'No fair. Why'd she do that? They usually at least wait until I've introduced myself.'

Cally patted her partner's shoulder reassuringly. 'Keep fishing, handsome.'

Eddie slouched into silence while Cally continued to survey the crowd for Ken Ho. After a couple of minutes, she saw a man approaching them, a man who looked exactly as smiling-eyed and plump-cheeked as his holo-gram back on the Deveraux Selector Agent database, if perhaps a little rounder of girth. 'Mr Ho?' she hazarded.

'Ken,' the man nodded. 'Ken Ho. And you're Cally and Eddie.'

'Eddie and Cally, actually,' muttered Eddie.

'Sorry I've kept you waiting. Punctuality in airlines proves that miracles are not dead.' Ken Ho's eyes twin-kled. Cally liked him. 'Wheelless is right outside if you'll follow me, please.'

They did. Eddie wasn't really paying much attention to what their contact was saying, however – the niceties about flights and how hotel accommodation was an unnecessary drain on Deveraux resources when there was plenty of room in his own apartment with only himself and his daughter living there since his wife died . . . Eddie was keeping a look-out for the black-haired girl in the floral dress. Maybe she was shy. Maybe he should have just kind of winked at her instead of making a move and if he could only glimpse her again . . .

Maybe she'd been talking to *Bex*.

It was too late now, anyway. They were outside in the blistering heat and the concrete glare and the honk of impatient vehicles.

And Ken was still . . . *what* was he saying? 'Sent my daughter in to find you while I parked the wheelless. Soon as she did she came running back out . . .'

'Daughter?' Eddie seemed suddenly awake.

'My daughter Kiri.' A proud father. 'She's waiting for us in the wheelless.'

So she was. Kiri was the black-haired girl in the floral dress.

'I just don't reckon we'll get any useful info out of Mrs Bain,' Bex complained as she and Ben were SkyBiking through a select residential area north of San Diego. 'I reckon she's shot away – she looked awful on the videphone.'

'Well that's a typically caring way to talk about someone who's probably just lost her husband,' commented Ben, checking the bike's navigator. A few more minutes and they'd be at the Bain residence.

'What? The husband we've put in the frame for blitzing Solartech and frying all those people? If that's true she's well out of it.'

'You don't sound convinced.'

'How can you tell?' snorted Bex. 'Nah. Me, I reckon

this entire Bain thing's a waste of our time. Scientists don't go in for sabotage or techno-terrorism. That's too exciting and they're too boring.'

'Boring's bad, huh?'

'Badder. You've got to stand out, Ben, don't you reckon? You've got to be distinctive somehow, make your mark.' Bex sought for words. 'Conformity is coma.'

'So is this why the hair and the piercings?' Ben was interested and mildly amused at the same time. 'I can see how *they're* going to make their own mark.' Bex flashed him a sarcastic smile. 'So all Eddie needs to do is invest in a nose-ring and some green hair dye and he might be in the running again.'

Bex waggled her finger admonishingly. 'One word more in *that* direction, Ben, ex-team leader or not, and I will continue this journey in silence.'

'Suit yourself,' Ben said. 'Journey's over.'

The Bain house was set back from the road, stylish yet traditional, built in solid timber and boasting several gabled bedrooms. Ben and Bex parked their SkyBikes, walked together to the door.

'Okay,' said Ben, 'you keep her talking and I'll have a quick look around.' He rang the bell.

'Hold on,' protested Bex, 'why don't *you* keep her talking and *I'll* have a quick look round?'

'Because, Rebecca, as you correctly pointed out a moment ago – ' Ben rang the bell again – 'I *am* a former team leader and so I outrank you in the field.' He rang a third time. They could hear the bell echoing through the house, but it was an empty kind of echo. It suggested absence. 'This is the time we arranged, isn't it?'

'Like I said,' Bex noted, 'shot away.'

'Well if Mrs Bain's out, we're in.' Ben produced a deactivator from his belt, placed it over the door's electronic lock. 'So now neither of us needs to keep her talking and we can both have a quick look around.'

The door clicked open. Ben and Bex slipped inside, eased it closed behind them.

Nothing appeared out of the ordinary. There was a hallway, stairs, rooms to right and left. But that was one of the first lessons they'd learned at Spy High: never trust the ordinary.

Particularly when, in a house where nobody answered the door, the videvision was still on.

Laughter from a studio audience led the Bond Teamers into a lounge. An empty lounge, except for a glass of water on a table by an armchair facing the screen and ready to be drunk.

Bex looked quizzically to Ben. 'I've got a bad feeling about this,' he breathed quietly. 'Through there.' Indicating a second door, this one tantalisingly ajar, as if inviting the intruders further into the house. Like walking into a trap, Ben thought. Bex wished they'd brought shock blasters with them.

But there was no alternative. They moved on.

Mrs Bain was waiting for them in the kitchen. It was a modern, spacious kitchen, where many delicious meals had no doubt been prepared. Mrs Bain wasn't going to be making further contribution in that regard though. She was lying on her back on the tiled floor. Her mouth was open but she wasn't breathing and her eyes were open but she couldn't see. It was unlikely she'd have heard the bell.

'Ben.' Bex's voice was ice. She wasn't looking at the body.

Ben followed the direction of her stare and he saw it
too.

Even the most rudimentary knowledge of incendiary
devices would have been sufficient to identify it: a bomb,
basic but deadly. And set on the kitchen table like the
latest creation of a peculiarly psychotic chef. It was a
bomb operated by a remote-controlled timing mechanism. And it was only seconds from detonation.

Cally reclined on Ken Ho's sofa and wondered what
Ben was doing right now. She was finding herself
thinking about him quite a lot lately. Part of her wished
she'd been teamed with Ben now, though another part
of her considered that that was being unfair to Eddie.
Not that Eddie would be unduly distressed if she left
the room just at the moment, she wagered. He probably wouldn't even notice. His eyes were welded to
Kiri Ho.

'I've never met a real secret agent before,' Kiri was
saying. She was kneeling on the floor gazing up at
Eddie with something like adoration.

It was close enough for him to fancy his chances. 'We
tend to keep a low profile,' he said. 'That's where the
secret part comes in.'

Kiri laughed. Eddie couldn't believe his luck. 'When I
saw you at the airport, I didn't have the courage to
approach you, knowing who you were.'

'That's crazy. We might be, you know, risking our
lives every day for the good of humanity, but when it
comes down to it, we're just ordinary guys doing a
job.' Eddie was modesty personified. 'And me in particular, I'm very approachable. You can get as close to

me as you like.' Kiri wriggled on the floor. 'Closer than that.'

Cally sighed from the other side of the room. Ken Ho had left them to make themselves at home while he quickly concluded some business. She hoped that quickly would be right.

'I know what my father does for you,' Kiri was revealing. 'I know about your school. It sounds so exciting.'

'Well,' Eddie brushed the excitement away as he would a fly, 'you get used to it after a while, you know what I mean?'

'I wish I could have joined Spy High.' Her eyes entreated. 'Do you think I could have made a secret agent like you, Eddie?'

'Maybe. I could give you a bit of an examination to find out.' Cally rolled her eyes.

'I know some judo,' Kiri claimed. 'My father taught me. He says a girl always ought to know how to defend herself in case a boy tries to take advantage of her.'

'How true,' Cally concurred.

Eddie glared.

'Can I show you?' pressed Kiri, jumping to her feet.

Eddie brightened. 'Sure,' he said, standing too. They moved to the centre of the room. 'Okay, so what did your Dad teach y—'

He suddenly found himself on his back and on the floor.

'Throws,' Kiri answered. 'I'm so sorry, Eddie. Weren't you ready for that?'

'A good secret agent,' groaned Eddie, 'is ready for anything.'

'Maybe judo practice should wait,' Cally said, amused

though she was. She'd heard the door. 'Sounds like your dad's back, Kiri.'

For the first time since they'd met him, Ken Ho was not smiling. 'I have some information,' he said, his expression dark with anger. 'Craven is here, in Honolulu. His private jet landed an hour ago.'

'Any idea of his plans?' Cally asked.

'Not exactly. Though it seems he will be present to watch the Oahu Cup tomorrow and to award the prize.' If anything, the man's mood grew bleaker still.

'What's the Oahu Cup?' Eddie wanted to know, having assumed a sitting position and otherwise appearing quite happy on the floor.

Kiri surprised both he and Cally by speaking out. 'It's an AquaBike race,' she said, 'around the island itself. It used to be a chance for the people to show off their AquaBiking skills. It used to be a wonderful occasion that everybody loved.' Her brow furrowed to match her father's.

'Then Craven Industries stepped in to sponsor it,' Ken Ho continued, 'and now it's a way of putting us in our place. A Craven employee wins every year, by whatever means possible, fair or foul, and because so many jobs on the island now depend on the man, nobody complains. We simply let it happen. We don't stand up for ourselves.'

'What are our chances of getting close to Oliver Craven while he's here, Ken?' said Eddie.

Ken shook his head – minimal.

'Then maybe it's time we gave this Oahu Cup thing a bit of a twist. Mine and Cally's bikes got shipped in, didn't they?' A slow smile spread across Ken Ho's face.

Eddie gave his hand to Kiri and she pulled. 'Maybe it's time somebody stood up to Oliver Craven, after all.'

They made the lawn but they didn't make their bikes. The blast hit them like a solid wall, swatting them forward and pitching them flailing to the grass. Its force was so great that Ben's jacket was torn off over his head. They hit the ground hard, but that was okay. As splinters and shards of timber and glass sliced jaggedly through the air, cutting the peaceful afternoon to shreds, the Bond Teamers would have been in a far more dangerous position had they been standing.

'Cover your head!' Ben barked.

'Who appointed you Stater of the Obvious?' Bex shot back. She was already in advance of Ben on that one.

The debris of the explosion dropped like litter. The sound of the detonation itself faded and was replaced by the less intimidating crackle of flames. Ben rolled over, got to his feet and dusted himself down.

'You okay?'

'I've been worse.' Bex gazed at the blazing ruin of the Bain house. 'Guess I was wrong before. Wastes of time tend not to get you nearly blown up.'

'Right,' agreed Ben. 'So Bain's involved, but whether this was him covering his tracks – messily – or whether he's as much a goner as his wife, that's another matter.'

Bex turned her attention to the nearest houses. Their owners stood nervously in doorways, watching their neighbour's place burn. They all seemed ready to dart back inside and lock their doors at a moment's notice. Nobody made the slightest move to help. 'Nice neighbourhood. Hope somebody's at least called the cops.'

Something more immediate had occurred to Ben. 'Bex . . . that bomb. With that kind of remote control, it has to have been activated by someone close by.'

A single wheelless that had been innocently parked a hundred yards down the road, too far to be associated with the Bain home, was suddenly moving, accelerating. It was heading their way.

'I see what you mean,' gulped Bex. 'Er . . . evasive manoeuvres?'

The wheelless left the road and sped across the lawns *directly* towards them.

'No way,' snarled Ben. 'You don't get a Stanton running away twice in one day.'

He raised his arms. His wrist-bands gleamed. Ben sprayed sleepshot at the oncoming wheelless. The shells struck like flints at the vehicle's windscreen, cracking, chipping, webbing the glass with fissures. Bex added her own fire to Ben's. The wheelless's driver was finding his machine hard to control, swerving from side to side. One more burst of shells and the windscreen shattered entirely. Bex could see the driver, the only occupant of the vehicle, flinging up his hands to protect his face. Without having engaged the automatic driving function.

The wheelless spun wildly. Ben consented to leap out of its way, though he clearly resented having to hit the dirt a second time. The vehicle ploughed into the Bain garden like a rogue rotovator, showering up the soil, biting deep into the ground before finally coming to rest.

There was no movement from within. Ben took no chances. 'Cover me!' he commanded. With his right hand ready to renew the sleepshot barrage, he flung wide the driver's door with his left.

Bex relaxed. 'I don't think we're gonna have to worry about *him*.'

The mysterious driver was slumped back in his seat, his skin an unhealthy shade of white, perhaps due to whatever substance it was that the man had evidently consumed and that was now frothing blackly at his still twitching lips. The rest of him was motionless and certain to remain that way.

'Two bodies on the same mission,' Bex totted up grimly. 'Maybe we're getting group rates.'

Ben leaned across the corpse and retrieved a small control device from the passenger seat. 'This is our bomber all right, though,' he said.

'Pity he's not going to be able to tell us anything,' said Bex.

'Oh, forensics'll make him talk.' Ben seemed confident. 'But I thought swallowing poison to prevent capture went out with the Cold War. You need to be either a fanatic or extremely scared of failing your employer to do something like that.' He looked at Bex meditatively. 'Maybe this Craven guy's more formidable than we thought.'

An estimation that might well have been reinforced had Ben had visual access to a certain stealth satellite high above the earth, a satellite which had been launched from Craven property mere months ago, a satellite from which he and Bex were now under careful and constant surveillance.

The diner had seen better days and if Lori had been travelling with her parents they wouldn't have contemplated stopping there for a second. Today, though, as the afternoon wore towards evening, she was with Jake, and he insisted. At least they'd be served quickly. Apart from the staff – chef, waitress and a woman behind the counter – there were only two other people present: a man in a booth hidden by the paper he was reading and an old-timer balanced precariously on a stool, slobbering toothlessly at a mug of coffee. Lori selected the booth nearest the door, as if she envisaged the possible necessity for a quick getaway.

'Can I getcha somethin'?' The waitress seemed to resent doing what she got paid for.

'Just coffee, please,' said Lori. 'Decaf.'

Jake ordered steak, eggs, fries and onion rings. 'And real coffee,' he added. 'Plenty of caf.'

Lori pulled a face. 'Do the words healthy eating mean nothing to you?'

'You're right, Lo,' Jake conceded. 'Can I have a side salad with that as well, and you'd better make it a low-fat dressing.'

'When you start to bloat, Jake,' Lori warned, 'don't be surprised if I leave you for another man.'

'And I thought you loved me for my mind.'

'Hmm.' Lori looked around at the peeling paint and patched leather, the unwiped stains of yesterday's meals. 'So what part of your mind decided we should break our journey here, then? Littleport's only another few miles up the road. We could have been there by now.'

'Exactly,' said Jake. 'And then we'd have been switched straight into secret agent mode, doing our thing to save the world.'

'Is that bothering you?'

'No. Course not. But I just wanted one last moment of

the two of us being ourselves, with time to ourselves, before the mission takes over entirely.'

'That's nice, Jake.' The waitress arrived with their food. 'Wish I could say the same for your cholesterol platter.'

'Don't you think,' Jake pursued, digging in, 'don't you think the one downside to the work we do is how it controls nearly every part of our lives? You know, controls what we do, where we go, even how we relate to other people. I can never tell anyone who isn't at Deveraux the truth about my life, not even my own family. Not that Pa'd be interested anyway.'

'I never thought of it like that,' mused Lori. 'I suppose it's just something we'll have to get used to. That's why it's so important to trust your team-mates, I guess, and maybe, in some special cases, more than trust them.' She smiled shyly. 'I'm glad we stopped here, Jake. You're right. A little time to ourselves . . .'

' 'Scuse me. You kids. 'Scuse me.' The old-timer had somehow slipped from his stool and kind of fallen against their table. 'I wasn't listening. I wasn't listening. But I heard the young lady say you was headin' for Littleport.'

Jake and Lori exchanged glances and sighed. Interlude over.

'That's right,' said Lori politely, 'but we're riding SkyBikes, so if you're after a lift . . .'

The old man shook his grizzled head vigorously, almost unbalanced himself. 'Don't go there. Don't go there, is what I'm saying.'

'Why?' Jake didn't know whether to be annoyed by the old man's intrusion or intrigued by his information.

'The lights, see. It's the lights. I saw them.' Eyes wide, it was as if he was seeing something now.

'What kind of lights?' Lori probed.

'In Littleport. The lights. I was there then. I saw them. I know.' He shook his head again, lips flapping, spittle stained with coffee. Then he was thrusting his head forward, lurching closer to the teenagers, almost confidential. 'The lights'll get you if you don't watch out.' And with that he staggered towards the door.

Jake sat still and reflective for a moment. 'Did that really just happen, or did we imagine it?'

There was more movement in the diner. The man with the paper had evidently finished it. He was striding past, also keen to leave.

'Drunk and old and mad,' was Lori's verdict.

'Very,' Jake agreed, 'on all three counts. But I'd like to know what the heck he thought he was talking about.'

'Nothing. Lights?' Lori shrugged. 'Probably delusional from the drink.'

'Yeah . . .' said Jake, not sounding totally sure, 'but let's get the old guy to explain himself anyway. Come on. He's probably collapsed in a heap right outside the door.'

He wasn't. There was no sign of the old drunk anywhere, only the man with the paper standing by a wheelless and lighting up a cigarette.

Lori frowned. 'Maybe he had a wheelless and drove off, though I'm pretty sure there was only that one car here when we arrived.'

'Maybe the lights got him,' Jake suggested with a grin. 'Either way, drunk, old and mad is unavailable for further questioning. Let's go back inside, Lo. I've still got some heart disease to work on.'

The man with the paper watched them re-enter the

diner. He was still there to watch them come out again twenty minutes later and resume their journey. Only when it was clear that the two SkyBikes were headed in the direction of Littleport did he get into his own vehicle and start the engine.

And by then the feeble thumps and muffled cries from the wheelless's boot had ceased.

FIVE

The old drunk from the diner had been right about one thing. It probably wasn't a good idea to go to Littleport, at least not if you were looking for anything like a fun time. If the town had been a body, by now the paramedics would have been attempting to resuscitate it.

Lori and Jake were loitering by the harbour. Darkness had settled in for the night and made itself comfortable. The silhouettes of a handful of forgotten fishing boats bobbed forlornly on black waters. If they'd been inclined, the Bond Teamers could have shouted out Spy High's inner-most secrets and it would have done no harm. There was nobody around to hear them.

Perhaps it was a coincidence that Deveraux seemed out of range as well.

'There's *still* something wrong with this communicator.' Lori fumbled at her belt with annoyance. 'All I'm getting is some kind of static. What about you?'

'The same,' Jake shrugged. 'Maybe they didn't get the proper safety checks before we left school.'

'Every agent's equipment *always* gets safety-checked before a mission,' Lori asserted.

'Don't look at me. I'm just a student.'

'I suppose it doesn't much matter,' frowned Lori. 'I can't see why we'd need to contact Deveraux anyway. I think the only danger we'll be in here is dying of boredom.' She sighed. 'Back to the guest house, then?'

'Hold on, Lo.' Jake's sharp eyes had glimpsed a shadow darker than the rest. 'I spy a local. So people *do* live here.'

Lori saw him too. A man standing in a doorway – her first instinct was to think *lurking* in the doorway, but that was probably unfair. A man with a pale smudge for a face, features indistinguishable in the paltry light, watching them like a ghost.

'Hi!' Jake called across. 'We're new in town and were kind of wondering . . .' The man obviously wasn't interested in what Jake and Lori were wondering. He stepped backwards and the darkness drowned him. 'Okay,' Jake muttered. 'That's somebody who doesn't work in community relations. Looks like it's the guest house after all, Lo.'

They'd checked in earlier. The large white clapboard house hadn't exactly impressed them as the obvious place to stay, but as it had turned out to be the *only* place to stay in Littleport, Lori and Jake were having to make the best of it.

Lori had already broached with the proprietor the subject of Oliver Craven. 'I've read so much about him,' she'd claimed, passing over the fact that she'd also escaped nearly certain death at the local hero's hands. 'Did you know him when he lived here? What's he like? It must be so exciting, knowing someone famous.'

Mrs Carver had not appeared unduly elated, though her lips had curled slightly in the hint of a smile. 'Mr Craven is a great man,' she'd said. 'A very great man.'

'What about his family, his parents?' Lori had enthused. 'Do they still live in Littleport?'

'Mr Craven's parents are dead.' The smile hadn't lasted long, replaced by an expression devoid of emotion, like the drawing of blinds across a window.

Lori hadn't persisted with her inquiries. A tourist's routine curiosity was one thing, but she hadn't wanted to suggest any ulterior motive. She'd simply signed the visitor's book as Lori Avon and let Mrs Carver lead them to their rooms.

Which was one advantage of the place being virtually deserted. She and Jake had each been given family rooms. Now, as they returned from their walk to the harbour, they were standing outside hers.

'Guess we may as well turn in early, then,' Jake said, though showing little sign of heading to his own room.

'Guess so.' Lori toyed with the key in her hand.

'You going to be all right?'

'I've slept on my own before.'

'Yeah, well, I'm just down the hall if . . .'

'If what, Jake?'

'Well, if you need me. You know. For anything.'

'I know. Thanks.'

'Yeah, right. Well, I guess it's bed then. Give the place a good going over tomorrow.'

'Tomorrow. So.' Key in lock. Lori turned it. Jake watched. 'Looks like I'm in.'

'Looks like it.' The door eased open and Lori turned on the lights. Jake peered inside. 'You want me to just kind of . . .'

'What?' Lori chuckled. 'Check if there's a ninja in the closet? A psycho in the shower?'

'I could keep watch for you.'

'Goodnight, Jake.'

'Goodnight? Okay, goodnight it is.' Jake seemed resigned. 'But hey, Lo, I know in public we're brother and sister on this little SkyBike trip, but we're not in public now, are we? No one's looking.'

'Looking at what?'

'This.' He leaned forward and kissed her. Lori didn't object. ''Fraid whenever you're around, Lo, I don't feel too brotherly.'

'Good*night*, Jake.'

But later, when she was alone, Lori kind of wished he'd stayed. There was something about Littleport, about the humourless Mrs Carver, the empty streets, the phantom locals, that made her uneasy. It extended to her room, too. She wouldn't tell Jake, but she had checked the closet – ludicrously – before she slipped into bed, though for what she had no real idea. And still she felt strangely vulnerable. It wasn't a Spy High team leader feeling at all.

Maybe some reading might help relax her. Lori opened the drawer in the bedside cabinet, expecting to find some tourist literature or perhaps a Gideon's Bible. Instead she found a children's novel, a single crease as deep as a frown across its cover, as if the book had once been dropped in haste. She picked it up anyway, flicked through it. Written on the first page in a child's blackish letters: 'Hands off! This book belongs to Tommy Nicholls'.

Poor Tommy Nicholls, Lori thought. Not only had he once had to stay at the Littleport Bed and Breakfast, but he'd left his book behind as well. She wondered where he was now.

'We don't know.' The tech shook his head in unaccustomed bafflement. 'At the present time, we just don't know.' He indicated the screen set into Senior Tutor Grant's smart-desk, the constantly changing and combining sequences of symbols that were displayed on it. 'It's language, sir, but not as we know it.'

Ben shifted restlessly on his chair. 'You mean the Babel chip can't translate it? What about our cryptographers?'

'Not so far,' admitted the tech reluctantly. 'Of course, that doesn't mean they *won't* . . .'

Bex interrupted. 'But I thought Babel technology could translate any known language going back, I don't know, to ancient Sanskrit or something.'

The tech looked too embarrassed to reply, so Mr Grant substituted for him. 'That's true, which rather implies that the writing on these files that Lori located is *not* in any known language.'

'Great,' grumbled Ben. 'That's just great.'

After the cops had arrived at the remains of the Bain house, there'd been little for Ben and Bex to do but return to Spy High as quickly as possible. That had been yesterday, and Ben for one had not been happy that their contribution to the mission seemed to have gone up in smoke quite so soon and quite so literally.

He was scarcely in a better mood now, as Grant updated them on developments in his study. 'What about the guy who tried to kill us?' he asked. 'Any leads there?'

'Oh, we know who he is,' Grant said. 'A minor criminal, someone who seemed to have dropped out of circulation about a year ago. What we don't know is the exact nature of the poison he took. It's deadly, obviously, but according to preliminary analysis, its chemical composition can't be matched to any other poison on our database, and I don't have to tell you how familiar we are with a significant range of fatal substances.'

'Where's Sherlock Holmes when you need him?' Ben muttered. He was thinking brick walls, brick walls all around him and his team-mates on the other side accomplishing great things without him. Best in School was fine, but Best on Mission was better.

Maybe Bex was thinking the same. 'How are the others doing, sir?'

Grant dismissed the tech before he replied. 'We haven't actually heard from Jake and Lori,' he said. 'There seems to be a problem with their communicators. And, as you know, use of spy lenses in the field has been temporarily suspended while we make them a little more robust.'

'I guess they can call in by vid if they need to,' said Bex.

'Exactly. It seems unlikely that Littleport is going to tax their resources. As for Eddie and Cally,' Grant ran his hands through his hair automatically as he said Eddie's name, 'they've made contact with our Agent in Hawaii as planned. It seems that Craven himself is in

Honolulu just now, so they've got plenty to keep themselves occupied.'

Yeah, right, Ben brooded darkly. So the others get the glory while he was stuck back here at Spy High. Not that he minded a little glory going Cally's way, or even Lori's, but Jake and Eddie . . . It was bad enough during the mission to the Temple of the Transformation, but to be left behind again, holding the fort, that was unacceptable.

'So what are Ben and I going to do now, sir?' Bex asked.

There had to be something. And then, of course, thinking of the Temple, Ben realised what it was. 'I know,' he said. He wasn't looking forward to it but anything was better than twiddling his thumbs while others flexed their muscles. 'I know where we might learn something about Oliver Craven.' Craven *had* to have been a member of the Centennial Club, maybe a participant in the whole Life Force Transfer scam. Mega-rich madmen tended to stick together.

'Yes, Ben?' Senior Tutor Grant prompted.

'From my so-called uncle.' Ben's tone was bitter. 'Alexander Cain.'

As it turned out, the organisers of the Oahu Cup were only too pleased to accommodate Edward Nelligan as a late entry for the event. How could they turn down the former European Under-Eighteen SkyBike champion, in Hawaii and prepared to race? Especially as, just that morning, they'd had an unexpected withdrawal – a local rider called, oh, yes, Brett Ho – he'd apparently fallen and done himself some damage, so it couldn't be more convenient. Eddie would be riding as number forty-one.

'This is gonna be a doddle, a walk in the park, like taking candy from a baby.' Eddie's modesty was wonderful to behold. Kiri Ho, keeping close to his side as they made their way to the jetty where the entrants' AquaBikes were waiting, seemed to be finding *him* wonderful to behold. Cally hoped that Eddie would be able to keep his mind on the race. 'Don't look like that, Cal. Craven's boys won't know what's hit them.'

Ken Ho, completing the quartet, did not appear optimistic. 'There they are,' he pointed out with a scowl. 'Craven's racers.'

There were three of them, climbing on to their AquaBikes further along the jetty. Arrogance emanated from them like bad breath. They looked like thugs and their sallow faces contorted into dismissive jeers as they regarded their rivals, particularly those who were clearly local. None of the three were Hawaiian.

'That's Jim Tanner.' Ken Ho identified the middle rider, a powerful-looking man with a bristling moustache. 'He's the real danger. He's won the race the last two years and he's after the same again. The other two are basically outriders. If anyone gets too close to Tanner, they'll take him out.'

'Really?' Eddie tipped Kiri a wink. 'Guess I'd better go and introduce myself, then.' He swaggered towards Jim Tanner.

'Eddie,' Cally called after him, 'don't do anything stupid.' But she was wasting her breath as always.

'Hi,' Eddie announced himself boldly, earning the immediate and suspicious attention of three sets of eyes, all of them cold. 'I understand you're Jim Tanner, the man to beat.'

'And who might you be?' Tanner's response was not friendly.

Eddie smiled anyway, bright-eyed and bushy-tailed. 'I'm the boy who's gonna whip your ass, big guy.'

'Why, you—' Goon One grabbed for Eddie and made a fist, but Eddie was already back-peddling blithely and giving the Craven men a little wave. Goon Two looked like he might lunge after him, but Tanner held his arm. All that pursued Eddie back to his companions was a glare.

'I hope you know what you're doing,' Ken Ho said.

'If I don't,' said Eddie, 'nobody else will. Let's race.'

The line that would mark both the start and the finish of the Oahu Cup was strung between two platforms which floated out on the waters beyond Waikiki beach. The AquaBikes idled their engines and waited for the starter to wave his flag. At a respectful distance from them the sea was studded with other AquaBikes, with boats large and small, even a number of outrigger canoes. All were packed with onlookers, cheering and whooping, none of them for Jim Tanner or for Craven. But that didn't seem to concern the race favourite. Tanner was gazing around with disdain.

Eddie had positioned himself close enough to keep a good eye on his rival. At that moment there were some fifty participants in with a chance, but by the time Waikiki beach came in sight again, he expected there to be just the two of them.

'Riders, get ready!' The command from the starter.

Eddie gave a final glance landward. From the rostrum

that had been erected on the beach Oliver Craven was watching. Eddie intended to make it worth his while. *If only Bex was watching, too.* Eddie frowned, rejected *that* particular thought. He pressed his helmet down on his head and fixed his goggles over his eyes. Forget Bex. She wouldn't be thinking of him. If she was here, she'd probably be rooting for Tanner.

The flag was flourished. With a roar of revs and a cascade of spray, the Oahu Cup 2064 got underway.

Tanner was out of the blocks quickly, his companions on either side to prevent other riders from straying obstructively near, either by accident or design. Eddie could rely on no such assistance, but his own natural skills were enough to keep him unencumbered by the pack. A number of AquaBikes had shot ahead recklessly, with speeds that could not be sustained, riders looking for a moment of fame in leading the race, however briefly, no real expectation of winning. Eddie would catch those later. His immediate concerns were the slower machines and those that in the thrill of competition seemed to have lost their sense of direction. He weaved between them, angled past them, adjusting the nuances of his speed to slow or quicken as his manoeuvres required. His bike responded perfectly to his ministrations, did what he wanted almost before he knew he wanted it. *If only Bex was an AquaBike, he might have a* . . . No. *Still* don't go there. Go after Jim Tanner instead, and think of Kiri Ho waiting to congratulate you on your victory . . .

Eddie boosted his speed, splitting the waters open, and left the amateurs floundering in his wake.

Honolulu fell away behind them. As they began their

great circle around the island, the shores to their left grew wilder, untamed, a riot of tropical vegetation and plunging cliffs. Maybe this was the cue for the racers to forget the rules as well.

Somebody had the temerity to draw level with Jim Tanner. Immediately, Goon One changed his line and skimmed his bike directly at him. The impertinent rider didn't seem to care, thought that he could outrace the Craven man and take the lead. Maybe he could have done. Goon One didn't give him the chance.

He rammed the side of the other man's bike, Eddie saw him do it. No grace. No subtlety. Bare-faced intimidation. To the other man's credit, he didn't back off, not even when Goon One repeated the action. But he was struggling now to steer his bike, uncertain how to retaliate. Goon One didn't give him the chance to do that, either. Now, and in a move that Eddie had to concede was daring and brave in its own way, he leant across from his own speeding vehicle and, while the desperate rider clung to the handlebars, wrenched brutally at the navigator controls. At once the hapless AquaBike spun hard to port, careered in an arc that could not be sustained. Its front dipped, smashed into the sea. Its rider was flung howling over the handlebars. He'd be fine, but he'd also been removed as a threat to the favourite.

So they liked the rough stuff, did they? Eddie grinned to himself. Well, that was okay. So did he.

And it wouldn't be long in coming, either, he estimated. As predicted, the vast majority of competitors had now either reconciled themselves to defeat or decided that they didn't have the nerve to tackle Jim Tanner. By the time the bikes were turning back towards Waikiki beach, only Eddie was in any position to challenge the Craven man.

Time for Eddie to make his move.

His opponents' Craven-manufactured AquaBikes were good, but his Spy High machine had plenty to offer as well. Eddie lowered himself in the saddle, streamlining the bike further. He flipped the hidden catch in the handlebar, pressed the button for hyper-acceleration.

Just as well he was wearing protective goggles.

Eddie surged forward, his bike hardly even touching the water now. He was past Tanner, and waving (cautiously – he didn't want to hyper-accelerate himself into the drink). And then the burst of speed was ebbing away, its power designed to be blistering but brief. But that was good, as Goons One *and* Two – Eddie was honoured – detached themselves from Tanner and made him their focus instead. Because Eddie didn't just want to beat the favourite. He wanted to take the lackeys as well.

They were closing down on him like a pair of jaws. Eddie let them. He let Jim Tanner race ahead. First things first. Goon One was leering as he struck at Eddie's AquaBike from the left, Goon Two ready to ram him from the right. But they weren't dealing with any ordinary rider now. Eddie was more than able to fend off their attacks and retain control of his machine. They'd be forced into snatching at his navigator controls in a moment. A moment he didn't plan on permitting.

Spy High AquaBikes came in a range of colours and with a number of special features unavailable to the general public. Eddie judged it was time to employ one of them now.

The immobiliser capacity.

'Bye, boys!' Eddie laughed, and flipped another switch.

On the two lackeys' AquaBikes, the engines suddenly cut out. Their systems crashed. The same total mechanical and electronic failure would have affected any AquaBike within a radius of fifty yards of Eddie – all systems down, including the safety systems.

The two bikes reared up into the air and spiralled across the sky. Goons One and Two were hurled hectically from their saddles. They were like men trying to fly. They didn't make it. Goons and AquaBikes plunged back into the sea.

Eddie ignored their cries. As Waikiki opened up ahead of him, he had only one purpose in mind. To overhaul Jim Tanner.

No hyper-acceleration now. No tricks. He'd cheated the cheats, but now Eddie was going to win fair and square. His own AquaBiking skills against Tanner's. He was the better rider, faster, stronger. He knew it. He'd prove it.

He was gaining.

Eddie anticipated the flow of the current, didn't fight the ocean, slalomed like a skier atop the foam and spray. Tanner was panicking, glancing behind him, losing concentration. His bike was committed to a straight line, cutting raggedly across the swells that nearer to shore would form breakers, limiting his progress.

Eddie could see the fear of failure etched across Tanner's face. His moustache was twitching.

At the last moment, as Eddie breasted him, Jim Tanner tried one final gambit, a desperate, doomed collision.

Eddie was having none of it. He switched his direction

swiftly and decisively. The two bikes crossed with inches to spare, and inches were sufficient. Eddie *did* hear Tanner's curses, though not for long. He was down in the saddle, knees locked against the bike's body like he was giving it a loving hug. Tanner was behind him now, like an unpleasant task completed. Only victory ahead.

And as the cries of acclamation rose from the beach, from the flotilla of craft swarming around the finishing line, Eddie could even afford to slow a little, to salute the crowd.

They'd weighed him down with garlands so that the fumes of the flowers almost choked him, and if they'd slapped his back any harder he could have had them all arrested for assault. But Eddie was in a magnanimous and forgiving mood. Let the crowds enjoy themselves, clamour round him euphorically. It wasn't often they saw Craven Industries losing out, and in the presence of the man himself.

Eddie fought his way to the prize-giving rostrum. The Oahu Cup awaited him. So did Oliver Craven. The scorching temperatures of Hawaii had not had a beneficial effect on Craven's general dampness, and perhaps the white suit and shirt had been a mistake. Shaking his hand was like wringing out a wet flannel.

'Well done, Mr Nelligan,' said Oliver Craven. 'Well done indeed.' His words at odds with the barely contained anger in his pale eyes and thin lips.

'Well, we can't have one of your guys winning every year, can we, Mr Craven, sir?' Eddie's impudent grin was well-practised. 'As they say in England, that just wouldn't be cricket.'

'I don't play sport, Mr Nelligan,' informed Craven coldly, 'of any kind. In sport there is always the possibility of defeat, and I don't like to lose.'

'Looks like I've made your day for you, then, doesn't it?' goaded Eddie. The mics were not on at the moment. The people jostling at the rostrum could not hear what was being said. Eddie pushed his luck – now was his chance to provoke the industrialist into letting something slip. 'You must like swimming, though, mustn't you, Mr Craven, sir? What with you living on New Atlantis and everything. Though I guess you need to be careful in those waters, don't you? Go for a bit of a dip and you never know what you might find. Sharks, you know, sealed tanks, things like that . . .'

Craven leaned closer to Eddie. 'Enjoy your moment of triumph, Mr Nelligan,' he advised, 'while you can.'

SIX

Ken Ho seemed to have hired out the entire restaurant. Certainly, everyone crammed inside was riotous in their celebration of Eddie's Oahu Cup success: singing, dancing, drinking, sometimes all three at once. It was like a wilder kind of wedding reception, with the cup as the centrepiece instead of a cake. There was a top table, where the victor himself sat flanked by Kiri and Cally, basking in the general adulation. Ken Ho shared the table, too, as did a younger version of the Selector Agent, a nephew, apparently, name of Brett. If Brett Ho *had* fallen and done himself some damage, Honolulu's medical community deserved respect. There was no sign of injury now.

A casual onlooker might have thought that Ken Ho had won the race, the way he clasped the trophy to him and then hoisted it in the air for all to see. His face was flushed as he attempted with limited success to embrace both Eddie and the cup.

'You don't know what this means to us, Eddie,' he declared, in a voice rather more slurred than usual. 'To beat Craven, to humiliate him in front of all those people, to win back the Oahu Cup for the people of Oahu. Ah, this day will be long remembered.'

'I think some of us'll be a long time recovering from this night, as well,' observed Eddie as Ken Ho started to sway.

'Ah, thank you, Eddie,' Ken beamed, 'for giving us back our pride. Thank you. And you, too, Cally.' He groped along the table. 'Thank you, too.'

'You're welcome,' said Cally, perhaps a little frostily. She wasn't resenting the fact that Eddie was the centre of attention, though she was sure she'd have raced just as well, but this whole Oahu Cup thing was, after all, just a digression from the real purpose of their being in Hawaii. To discover what Oliver Craven was up to down here. She remembered diagrams of bombs – what if they'd now been taken beyond the blueprint? 'But Ken,' she said, 'maybe we shouldn't be here. While Craven's on Oahu . . .'

'He's not,' Ken Ho told her, suddenly seeming to sober up. 'Right after the prize-giving ceremony he took a helicopter to Molohalu. It's a small island he owns to the south. Craven Industries have been carrying out scientific research there for the past few months.'

'Then that's where we need to go,' Cally asserted, almost rising to her feet as if she meant immediately.

'It's all taken care of.' Ken Ho rested his hand on her shoulder. 'We'll sail out there tomorrow, take your AquaBikes with us, see what there is to see. *On* the sea.' Ken chuckled. His interlude of seriousness seemed to have run its course. 'Tomorrow, Cally. Tonight we party! The cup is back where it belongs!' And he was staggering off once more with the trophy above his head to prove it.

Cally sighed but settled back into her chair. Tomorrow it would have to be.

Alongside her, Kiri was whispering into Eddie's ear. 'Eddie, I want to leave.'

'What? Aren't you having fun?' Eddie was concerned. 'Are you sick?'

A shy smile crept across Kiri's features. 'I want to leave with you, go somewhere quieter. Outside, maybe?'

With the look in Kiri's eyes, there was no maybe about it. 'Sure.' Eddie smacked his knee against the table-leg in his haste to stand. 'Could do with a breath of fresh air myself.'

The two of them threaded their way across the floor. Most of the revellers were partying so hard they didn't even notice.

The Hawaiian night was hardly cool, but it was still more comfortable and certainly quieter strolling in the street than it had been in the restaurant. Kiri kept close to Eddie. He instinctively placed his arm around her shoulders. She was wearing a bold floral number like at the airport and she looked just as good now as then.

'You were so wonderful today, Eddie,' Kiri said.

'Yeah?' Eddie looked for irony but there was none. 'I mean, yeah, I guess I was. Kind of. I mean, you know, all in a day's work for a Spy High graduate.'

'What did you think of me earlier?' Kiri probed innocently.

Same as now, Eddie thought. Gorgeous. Available. *But not Bex.*

'As a secret agent, I mean. You'll have to go back to

your school soon, won't you? I'd love to come with you.
I'd give anything to do that.'

'It's dangerous,' Eddie said, though not wanting to disappoint her. 'Real spycraft, it's not all AquaBike races.
It's not like the movies.'

'You'd look after me, though, Eddie, wouldn't you?
You'd protect me.'

'Well, the idea is that you're kind of trained to look
after yourself.' Eddie gulped as Kiri's face drifted ever
nearer to his own.

'That's a pity,' breathed Kiri. 'Some things are much
better done with two.'

He was about to close his eyes for the kiss, about to let
it happen.

Then the shadows came alive.

'Kiri, watch out!'

Eddie yanked her to one side as a black-robed figure
leaped at them from the night. Its kick would have
decapitated Kiri if his reflexes had not been honed by the
Spy High combat programs.

In a moment he'd assessed the scene: the scarfed head,
the lower face also concealed, the cold, emotionless
eyes – a ninja. And not alone. The darkness coagulated
into three of them. This was no mugging, Eddie realised
grimly. More likely a little parting gift from Oliver
Craven.

He shielded Kiri with his own body, tensed for battle.
'Get inside!' he snapped. 'Get Cally.'

'No!' Kiri adopted a defensive stance next to him. 'I
can fight. I'm not a child.'

No time to argue. Eddie was already ducking under a
scything kick, springing up to strike at the first ninja's

torso. His blow was blocked and then he was having to dart sidewards as the second ninja attacked from behind. A flurry of fists. He fended them off. But fighting front and rear was not good.

Eddie dropped low. Dived. Rolled. As the first ninja followed him, thinking he could predict Eddie's movements, he lashed out with his leg from the ground and swept the ninja's from under him, heard the satisfying thud of an impact against concrete.

Now it was two against two.

The second ninja was quick and powerful, a frustrating combination. Eddie had to devote so much attention to defence that he could not begin to mount an attack of his own. Worse, he could see that, despite her evident judo skills, Kiri was no match for the third. He tried to reach her but his own assailant was blocking his path on a permanent basis. 'Kiri!' he yelled.

She might have responded had the ninja's arm around her throat not been restricting the action of her larynx. A choke was all she could utter. Her opponent's free fist was poised to pound at the tender and vulnerable area of her temple. The implication was clear to Eddie. He should surrender now.

'Okay. Okay.' He raised his hands. 'Just don't hurt her, right?'

His own foe's eyes glittered. Whatever his companion chose to do, he was not going to let Eddie escape without pain. Without rather a lot of pain, it seemed. The never walk again kind.

Eddie hoped he wasn't going to cry out.

Kiri's ninja did, however, as Cally thudded ruthlessly into his back and sent him pitching forward, loosening his grip on the Hawaiian girl. Her sudden intervention caused the remaining attacker to glance away from Eddie. That split second wavering of concentration that two years of training taught Spy High students to exploit.

Eddie exploited. With force. With fury. His fist would ache for the rest of the night.

He was at Kiri's side with Cally, Kiri coughing and massaging her neck. 'Are you okay? Kiri, are you all right?' It seemed that she was, or at least was going to be. 'Good to see you, Cal,' Eddie added.

'Craven Industries Ninja Division, I assume. Can't I let you out of my sight for a minute without you getting into trouble?' Cally scolded playfully.

'Sorry, Mum,' Eddie grinned. 'Guess you'll have to send me to bed early again.'

'Which by coincidence is kind of why I came looking for you,' explained Cally. 'We'd better be . . . Eddie!'

Sudden alertness once more. While the Bond Teamers had been talking, the ninjas had been recovering. Only this time they seemed not to be seeking further conflict. As Cally and Eddie looked on, they melted back into the shadows from which they'd come.

'Shouldn't . . .' Kiri's voice was hoarse. 'Shouldn't you go . . . after them?'

'Go after them?' Eddie felt his bruised knuckles. 'I'm hoping I'll never see those guys again.'

'Priorities, Kiri,' said Cally, 'and our first one is rest. Tomorrow we have an appointment in Molohalu.'

As the shuttle commenced its docking procedures, Bex Deveraux trusted that the pilot knew what he was doing and fixed her gaze on Ben in the seat next to her, rather than on the penal satellite looming in space ahead of them. Ben's eyes, though, were riveted on the prison, and the blue in them seemed darker somehow, and brooding, and to Bex it seemed that he wasn't so much seeing what was there now as envisaging a scene yet to come.

He's so uptight, Bex thought. Good-looking, yes, and fit, but always so kind of *intense*. Takes everything so seriously. Never really lightens up. Maybe he doesn't know how to. If he was an actor, for sure, Ben Stanton could play drama and tragedy without a second thought, but comedy, she imagined that would prove a problem. Eddie, on the other hand . . . Bex stopped herself, mentally slapped her wrist. She'd made her opinion of Eddie clear and it wouldn't do to change her mind now, even if his presence *would* have livened up the shuttle journey. Anyway, Eddie was probably having a great time in Hawaii without her. He'd probably not given her a second thought since the mission started. And that was how she wanted it to be.

Green lights in the cabin announced that the docking had been successfully completed. 'Let's go.' Ben didn't grace her with a glance even now.

The next hour or so was going to be difficult for him, Bex accepted. The penal satellites had been born as a result of the overpopulation of prisons earthside and the resultant riots in the early years of the twenty-first century. At the time some politicians had declared that the only solution was to compulsorily lobotomise offenders and then return them to the community. Others, however, with certain notions of human rights in mind, had advocated a more humane approach. Send convicts with a sentence of over twenty years into orbit. Let them watch the world turning from the vantage point of a space station exclusively for criminals. Out of sight, out of mind. End of problem. One of the latest law-breakers to receive a one-way trip to the stars at the taxpayers' expense was Alexander Cain.

'You want one of my guards to come in with you?' the warden asked as he escorted Ben and Bex to the cell.

'I don't think that'll be necessary,' Bex smiled sweetly.

Ben simply grunted. His hands seemed permanently balled into fists.

'Well, the prisoners are under constant video surveillance,' the warden said. 'If Cain makes a wrong move, we'll know about it instantly.'

'He's already made a wrong move,' smarted Ben. 'Can you just open the door?'

'Please,' added Bex, not wishing to offend.

The cell might have belonged to any prison on earth, or a room in a very cheap hotel. The only feature which betrayed its location was the view from the window: the blackness of space, a spill of stars, the distant rim of the globe itself. There were no bars on the window. No prisoner who required oxygen to live was going to be breaking out that way. But perhaps Alexander Cain thought differently. As Ben and Bex entered his cell he was standing at the window with his back to them, his palm pressed almost tenderly against the specially re-inforced glass.

'Uncle Alex.' Ben said the name as if he was swearing in church. 'We're here.'

'So you are, Ben, so you are.' Alexander Cain turned to face them. Neither his austerely handsome features, nor his arrogant assumption of superiority seemed affected by his incarceration. Perhaps there were a few more grey hairs at the temples, but that was all. 'I would offer you both some refreshment but my ability to entertain guests has been somewhat curtailed by circumstances. I'm sure you understand.'

'We're not here to make polite conversation,' said Ben. 'Just tell us what we want to know and we're gone.'

'So soon, Ben?' Cain lamented with a sly grin. 'And there was a time when you used to actively seek my company.'

'That was before I knew what kind of man you are.' Ben was unable to hide his bitterness. Cain saw it and appeared refreshed. 'I wouldn't be here at all if you'd cooperated over the vide-link. It makes me sick sharing the same air with you.'

Cain chuckled. 'Ah, but visitors are so rare up here, you know. I couldn't resist the opportunity.' His eyes flickered to Bex. 'But this is Rebecca Deveraux, is it not? What happened to the lovely Lori, Ben? Is she still seeing that Neanderthal with the black hair? Nothing so conventional for you, I notice – ' indicating Bex's blue – 'but how does it feel, my dear, to be second choice?'

'Don't push your luck, Cain,' warned Bex.

'No games, Uncle Alex.' Ben paced the cell impatiently. 'Are you going to talk Craven or not? Right now, I'm ready to leave you here to rot either way.'

'Ah, but surely if you did that, Ben, you'd be failing in your duty,' Cain goaded, 'and I know how fundamental duty is to you, how you feel that championing the ignorant masses is more important than loyalty to your family's oldest friend . . .'

'Right. That's it.' Ben was at the cell door. 'Let's go.'

'Very well. Very well.' Cain shrugged nonchalantly. 'If you insist, I'll tell you what I know about Oliver Craven. For old time's sake, Ben. And besides, it will be nice to know you owe me a favour . . .'

It seemed that Oliver Craven had indeed been a member of the Centennial Club, and that his ruthlessness, callousness and total disregard for others had swiftly drawn Alexander Cain to him as like attracts like. It seemed that Cain had even invited the other man to be an active participant in the whole Temple of the Transformation charade. But it also seemed that Craven had turned the opportunity down. Flat. Not interested. And that before long he'd ceased attending the Centennial Club entirely.

'Oliver seemed always to have an agenda of his own,' Cain mused, 'though I was never able to determine the nature of his plans. As long as they did not interfere with mine, of course, I was scarcely concerned.'

'No ideas at all?' Ben said. 'That's unlike you.'

'Oh, ideas,' Cain acknowledged. 'I understand that Craven Industries has taken control of Douglas Elleray's Solartech company. That doesn't surprise me. Craven and our late mutual friend Hiro Nagashima often discussed the potential of solar power at the club. On one occasion, I remember, Hiro's industrial spies had reported that Elleray was diverting massive resources to a so-called Prometheus Project. Over-reaching himself, of course. It was there that Solartech's financial problems began.'

'Can we keep to the subject, Uncle Alex?' said Ben.

'As you wish. This Prometheus Project was so secret

that not even Hiro's men could learn much about it, and Hiro's men, as you can imagine, are very good at their job. If ever your organisation chooses to diversify into industrial espionage, Ben . . .' A silencing glare. 'No, I suppose not. So, all that could be ascertained was that somehow the Prometheus Project was connected to the creation of artificial suns. Elleray's idea was for these suns to be launched like rockets into the skies above hostile environments like Siberia, where the long winter darkness prevents the land from being cultivated, in order to improve the quality of life of the miserable peasants who inhabit such inhospitable regions. Bringing a little sunshine into their lives, so to speak. Well, naturally, Nagashima and I regarded any project for the benefit of others rather than ourselves with scorn and simply dismissed it. I recall Craven, however, growing rather excited about Prometheus technology, pressing Hiro for details that he did not possess. I imagine that this marked the commencement of his interest in purchasing Solartech.'

'And that's it, is it?' Ben scoffed. 'That's the best you can do? Artificial suns and the Prometheus Project? You'd better be careful, Uncle Alex. Prison's obviously addling your brains.'

'Bet you wouldn't turn your nose up at one of those artificial suns now, though, would you, Cain?' Bex joined in. 'It's gonna be a while before you feel the real one again.'

'Ah, the wit of youth,' Cain savoured. 'But before you go, one last thing. You must obviously believe Oliver Craven to be some kind of threat to your cosy little world or you wouldn't be here. I'd just like you to

know that whatever his agenda is, I wish him every
success. If it involves death and destruction, all the
better. And if he happens to harm you and your group
of noisome little friends playing your silly, secret agent
games at the same time, Ben – preferably fatally – then
I will applaud him from the heavens. Do you understand me?'

'That's just it, Uncle Alex,' said Ben coldly. 'I've *never*
understood you.'

It seemed that Littleport was almost as deserted by day
as it was by night. The few people Lori and Jake saw
shuffling about their business on the streets looked like
they could only barely remember what their business
was, and they walked with the uncertainty of long-term
invalids finally liberated from their beds.

The Bond Teamers made for the town library where
the town librarian sat in state and appeared to have been
recently mummified. She did, however, just about
manage to direct the teenagers to the bound sets of 'The
Littleport News' when requested. There were no computerised records here. If they wanted to research
Craven, they were going to have to sift hard copy in
order to do it.

'My God,' groaned Jake, papers piled before him.
'Who'd have thought a dead-end town like this could
generate so much *news*?'

'We can narrow it down to start with,' Lori said. 'Look
at dates around the time Craven first joined Ocean
Industries. That's where we could find our 'local boy
comes good' headlines. And Jake, don't panic. We've got
all day.'

'Lori,' moaned Jake, 'that's *why* I'm panicking.'

In the event, it took less than an hour for Lori to discover something she thought she ought to share. 'Look at this.' She beckoned Jake over. '"Littleport Lights. Fishermen report strange sightings at sea." Sound familiar?'

Jake furrowed his brow. 'Maybe that old drunk was on to something after all. What does it say?'

Lori read from the yellowing paper. '"Many are the myths of the ocean, from ravishing mermaids to terrifying sea monsters, but the crew of the trawler 'Lucky Blue' claim to have encountered something far more mysterious than the stuff of old seadogs' tales. It happened on Thursday night, as they sailed off Haven Point towards home. The sky was overcast and moonless. The sea was calm. There was no natural explanation for what occurred". Then it describes how the crew – all of them, mind you – saw these bursts of colour, white and red and yellow, like flashlights turning on and off, *under* the sea. Apparently, they kept on shining for several minutes, almost as if they were in pursuit of the boat, and then they vanished as quickly and as suddenly as they'd appeared.'

'Mass hallucination brought on by too long spent at sea?' Jake posited.

'Not according to Captain William Gallagher,' Lori said. '"Captain Gallagher denied his story was a trick or deceit in any way. 'I know what I saw,' he said. 'I know what my men saw. The lights were real. And I never want to see them again.'" And Jake, look!' Lori stabbed a photograph with her finger. 'Captain Gallagher, he's the drunk from the diner.' The picture was of a man far more presentable than the vagrant who'd accosted them the other day, but the features were essentially the same, nothing that several years of hardship couldn't have altered.

'You're right, Lo,' Jake agreed. 'Guess after that episode he found it difficult to keep fishing.'

'And the date of this paper, Jake,' Lori pursued, 'a month before Oliver Craven joins Ocean Industries.'

'What say we check if any more of Littleport's finest had problems with lights flashing before their eyes?' suggested Jake.

It seemed that some had. The 'Lucky Blue' incident turned out to be the first of a spate of light-sightings by vessels sailing near Haven Point. They occurred both by day and night, and always seemed to follow the same basic pattern. The episodes continued for several weeks. Lori found one article in which the town seemed on the brink of calling in a team of experts in supernatural phenomena to investigate. But then, just as abruptly as the ghostly lights themselves were reported to disappear, all mention of them in 'The Littleport News' ceased. Maybe it was because the townsfolk by that time had something else to talk about: 'Local Man Makes Name In Multi-National'.

'What do you think?' Lori asked.

'I think that I've got a terminal crick in my neck from leaning over library tables,' complained Jake, massaging that particular part of his anatomy. 'I think if I remain anywhere within seeing distance of said library tables or, indeed, of the library itself, I am going to scream and get us thrown out anyway. So all in all, I *think*, Lori, that we need a little relocation.'

'Any idea as to where?'

'Oh, yes,' said Jake. 'Haven Point sounds good to me.'

He'd spotted the boathouse on their way to the library. It jutted out on wooden legs over the harbour wall, and a slipway led from its very solidly closed doors to the sea when the tide was in, to the shingled beach when it was out. While the place had looked deserted, though no more so than anywhere else in Littleport, and the painted letters on its side were fading and flaking, the words they spelled out were still clear enough: 'Pleasure Cruises. All Parties Catered For. Rufus Mansfield, Proprietor'. Jake was hoping Rufus might be good enough to take them to Haven Point.

'Doesn't look like he's at work today,' Lori said. As Jake tried the doors to the boathouse for a fourth time. 'Maybe we can hire a boat somewhere else?'

'Maybe. Lori, is it me or can you smell something bad around here?'

'Forget the deodorant today?'

'No, I'm serious.' Jake wrinkled his nose in disgust. 'Something *bad*.'

'The salt air and rotting seaweed, I guess.'

Jake shook his head and was about to respond when he saw a weathered man in a striped sweater bearing towards them, a man with such prodigious amounts of facial hair that his skin could scarcely be glimpsed at all. Only his eyes. And they were not exactly sparkling with friendliness.

'What are you kids doing?' the man demanded. 'What do you want?'

'Mr Mansfield?' Jake said. It wasn't denied. 'We're a party of two. We'd like to hire your boat.'

Rufus Mansfield shook his head in short, emphatic motions. 'Boat's not for hire.'

'We can pay you.' Jake tried a disarming smile. 'We're wealthier than we look.'

'No.' Not even a sorry, however insincere.

'But your sign says —'

'Are you deaf, boy? Boat's not for hire.'

Lori wondered whether *her* charm might be a little more persuasive than her boyfriend's. 'Please, Mr Mansfield,' she all but simpered, 'I know it must be an imposition on you, but my brother and I would *really* appreciate it if you could see your way to . . .'

Jake clenching her wrist stopped her. 'Don't bother,' he advised.

'Boat's not for hire,' Rufus Mansfield repeated, like a mantra that was part of his soul.

And now Lori could notice what Jake had seen. Littleport residents, congregated in the harbour area in small groups, all silent, all watching the Bond Teamers and Mansfield. They'd come from nowhere. Lori didn't really want to think about why.

'Okay. We've got you. No problem,' Jake was apologising. 'Boat's not for hire. We're sorry to have bothered you. Bye. Thanks. Lori, after you.'

And as they moved away from the boathouse, so too did the good citizens of Littleport disperse and return to the routines of their day.

'What was that all about?' Lori pondered as they rushed back in the direction of Mrs Carver's. 'The way those people just *gathered*. Jake, what's going on?'

'I don't know, Lori,' Jake said darkly, 'but we're sure as heck going to find out. Soon as it gets dark we're going back to Mansfield's boathouse and we're taking a cruise. Whether he likes it or not.'

Black turned to blue as the shuttle containing Ben and Bex re-entered Earth's atmosphere. They'd be touching down in minutes.

'You okay now?' Bex ventured gingerly. Ben had been as uncommunicative on the return journey as he'd been during the flight *to* the penal satellite.

'Improving,' he gauged. 'The further I put Alexander Cain behind me the better.' But the memories – they were still there. Both of Uncle Alex's betrayal and before. And somehow, to Ben, it was the memories that *should* have been good, that should have been cherished but which with hindsight were now irredeemably tainted, that hurt the most. He wondered what the Deveraux policy was on selective mind-wiping.

'I know it must be hard,' Bex said, 'when someone you loved turns against you, when they seem like someone you don't know any more – ' she thought of her father, her dad the computer – 'but you mustn't let it get to you, Ben. I guess that's why he'd only speak to us face to face, don't you think? To see if he could still pull your strings?'

'Could be.'

'Don't let him, Ben. He's not worth it.'

'You don't need to worry about me, Bex,' Ben said with what was almost conviction. 'Like I said, I'll be fine. All I could do with right now is something to take my mind off Alexander Cain.'

A movement from outside the shuttle caught Bex's eye and she frowned. 'Maybe it's on its way,' she murmured. A second aircraft, larger than the shuttle but clearly equipped for high-altitude flying, was swooping with gleaming, predatory black wings towards them. 'Ben, do you think we're supposed to be this close?'

'It's coming right at us!' Ben was startled, urgent. 'Bex, it's attacking!'

SEVEN

For a moment it looked as if the two aircraft would collide, but at the last moment the black plane soared above the shuttle. Ben and Bex could no longer see it. They didn't have to. They knew that it was still out there.

The shuttle pilot's face appeared on the passenger cabin videscreens, struggling to stay calm, to exude authority. 'This is the captain. As you've no doubt noticed, an unidentified aircraft is currently flying dangerously close. Please remain seated while we attempt to make contact with the plane and establish the situation.'

'We've established,' muttered Ben, deactivating his automatic seat-belt. 'It may not say Craven Industries on the side, but this is about us. Has to be. Coming, Bex?'

'Coming where?' In a space shuttle, there weren't too many options.

'The cockpit. I think we need to let the captain know what's going on.'

The captain did not immediately welcome further company in the cockpit. He was a veteran of the satellite run and a firm believer that passengers and crew should be kept as separate as possible for security reasons. It was only his co-pilot's observations that their security was already jeopardised that persuaded him to relent and open the cockpit door.

'You mean you think they're going to shoot us down?' the captain quailed. 'But I own stock in Craven Industries.'

'If they wanted us shot down they could have done that already,' Ben reasoned. 'It's something else but I don't want to find out what. Get out that emergency signal now.'

'Now just hold on, sonny,' the pilot spluttered. Who did these kids think they were, joyriding to penal satellites, taking charge as if they had a right? He was a veteran of the satellite run . . .

'The plane's directly above us,' the co-pilot pointed out. 'I mean directly above us. It's shadowing our every manoeuvre.'

'All right,' the pilot consented. 'Emergency signal sending . . .'

Or not. Both pilots' faces paled in horror. All at once, as if they were victims of a sudden virus, every instrument in the cockpit failed.

'They've immobilised our systems,' Ben realised. 'We're sitting ducks.'

'Oh, my God. We're going to die. We're going to plunge to the ground and we're going to die.' And what a way for a veteran of the satellite run to go, the captain mourned.

'Keep those cheerful thoughts to yourself, Captain Brightside,' said Bex. 'We're not dead yet and me, I've got a crotchety old age to look forward to.' She turned to Ben. 'Distress call to Deveraux?'

Ben was already keying in the code in the appropriate segments of his belt. 'At least they'll know where to pick up the pieces. Now I assume we've got airsuits aboard . . .'

He was interrupted by a dull, heavy clanging against the roof of the shuttle. The craft shuddered like a man who'd just been knifed.

'My God, what's happening?' The pilot scrambled out of his chair and into the passenger cabin. 'Are we breaking up?'

The others followed. There were further muffled but metallic booms from above, like a hammer on a distant and titanic anvil.

'Is there somebody out there?' the co-pilot wondered. 'Is there somebody on the roof?'

'Ben?' Bex looked to the former team leader.

'They're going to board us.' Ben's tone almost suggested admiration. 'This is a skyjack.'

'We're not losing altitude.' Bex peered out of the window. 'Steady height, like we're being . . .' Her gaze passed to the roof, the steel there now seeming to dent and buckle, '. . . held in place. Clamped.'

The booming reverberated more loudly through the cabin, like artillery finding its range.

'Get down!' Ben cried.

He and Bex moved slickly. The Avoiding Sudden Explosions module in their mission training program had its benefits. The two pilots were slower. The force of the blast as the roof ruptured in two places threw them off their feet.

But the atmosphere inside the shuttle remained intact. No loss of oxygen or glimpse of naked sky. Twin tubes were now locked on to the craft, big enough for a man to pass through.

'Sleepshot ready,' Ben warned Bex. 'Use the seats for cover. You guys,' to the grovelling and startled pilots, 'get behind us. And stay *down*.'

'You don't have to tell us twice,' moaned the captain, who was kind of wriggling along on his uniformed belly like an overweight worm. The words Early Retirement were at the forefront of his mind, just behind Please, God, Let Me Out Of Here.

Ben and Bex were sculptures of concentration. No unnecessary movement now, not even blinking. From one or the other or both of the tubes that had punched their way into the shuttle, assailants would drop. Craven's men. Any second.

Any second now.

But instead, 'What's that?' Bex's sensitive hearing had detected a hiss, her nostrils the slightest change in the air. She knew what. 'Gas!'

They reached for their belt-breathers even as the pilots, in a kind of uncanny unison, made soundless shapes with their mouths, grabbed at nothing with their hands, and lolled into unconsciousness. There'd be no problem with getting them to stay down now.

Ben's belt-breather was fitted but maybe he'd been slow or maybe the gas had been pumping in even before they'd realised it. There was a fog in his mind. The cabin seemed to be elongating, made of elastic rather than metal, and his body, too. His hands seemed to be dangling at the end of arms like rubber. And dangling? What was the good of that? He needed to point. He needed to shoot.

Bex was calling his name. Or he thought she was. The sound crashed against him like waves on the rocks, syllables like spray. He thought he ought to smile at Bex.

There were more sounds. Like thudding on a door. Men in black, wearing helmets and carrying weapons were coming through the roof. And some of them were falling because Bex was pointing at them from behind a seat and Ben knew he ought to do the same thing but his hands seemed too far away to obey him and he was kind of swaying and he needed them to steady himself.

The new men weren't bothering with him. They seemed interested in Bex though, and why did she have to keep shouting at him? Oh, and then she wasn't. Then she'd gone to sleep. And now the new men were all around him and they seemed friendly because they were smiling.

Unusual when one of them was pointing a gun at him. And firing.

Eddie Nelligan leaned against the side of the motor-cruiser 'Aloha' and gazed out across the Pacific. He could almost read the brochure-speak: peaceful azure waters, endless days of tropical tranquillity, sky meeting sea in perfect harmony – come to beautiful Hawaii.

He doubted the island of Molohalu got a mention in

the holiday brochures, though. Tourists were probably not too interested in the schemes and depredations of Oliver Craven. And the scene as they sailed towards their destination might be calm now, but there was no way of knowing if it would remain that way. There'd certainly been ructions this morning before they'd set off.

All down to Kiri, really.

'What do you mean, I'm not coming?'

'This is Spy High work now, Kiri.' Cally had tried to explain. 'You're not trained for it. It'd be irresponsible for us to take you, particularly after last night . . .'

'Last night I held my own.' Kiri had conveniently forgotten the strangling arm around her neck.

'That's enough, Kiri.' Ken Ho had played the heavy parent for once. 'Cally's right. This is not a game, haven't you learned that yet? While we sail to Molohalu, you stay here.'

Which was when the moment Eddie had dreaded but had also known was inevitable had come, the direct appeal. 'Eddie, you'll let me go with you, won't you?' Those big, pleading brown eyes.

'Well, Kiri, actually, I know you can handle yourself but, well, Cal's kind of right. And your dad . . .'

Those big, *blazing* brown eyes. 'So that's what you think of me. A little girl who needs protection. That's what you really think of me. Well, thank you, Eddie. Thank you very *much*.'

And Kiri had rushed from the room. Leaving Eddie wincing: another one that got away.

He was still wincing now, intermittently, several hours into the voyage, and even as a smoky smudge on the horizon charcoaled itself into something a little more substantial.

'Molohalu!' called Ken Ho from the wheel.

'Doesn't look like much to me,' Eddie grumbled.

'Who's in a bad mood, then?' Cally teased, joining her partner at the handrail. 'Maybe a spot of underwater exploration'll cheer you up. And Ed,' she added more seriously, 'Kiri'll be there waiting for us when we get back, you'll see. Waiting for *you*.'

'Thanks, Cal,' Eddie said. 'If I need a cheerleader, I know where to come.'

'It's pretty much all volcano.' Ken Ho was still on the subject of Molohalu. 'Ninkini.'

'Bless you,' said Eddie.

'That's the volcano's name. Dormant, of course, but not exactly an encouragement for investment in tourism. Craven bought the island on the cheap.'

'That sounds right,' said Cally. She was beginning to see the accuracy of Ken's description. Molohalu was fringed with palm trees and beaches, a few grey and sober buildings she could make out, but the land swiftly rose into the towering, ominous hulk of the volcano.

'We've kept the site under surveillance since Deveraux's been investigating Craven,' the Selector Agent revealed. 'We've taken aerial photographs. There's nothing out of the ordinary as far as we can see.'

'Maybe you haven't been looking deep enough,' mused Cally, watching the sunlight play on the sea. She thought of Lori and the shark. 'We'll soon find out.'

'Hey, Cal,' Eddie alerted her. 'Try a little higher.'

Approaching them from Molohalu itself was a heli-copter. It was flying at speed and seemed to mean business.

'Don't panic,' said Cally. 'We're just innocent tourists out for a cruise.'

The chopper was hailing them as soon as it came within loudspeaker distance. 'You are approaching private waters.' The message was metallic, brooked no protest or compromise. 'This area belongs to Craven Industries. Please turn your boat around directly and continue your voyage elsewhere. Repeat: you are approaching private waters. Please turn around now.' The helicopter hovered above them, staining the sun.

'What do we do?' Ken Ho sought advice from his passengers.

'Exactly what they want us to,' decided Cally. 'And we smile and we wave while we're doing it.'

Eddie smiled and waved stupidly. 'Don't you just love this job?' he said.

Ken Ho spun hard on the wheel and the 'Aloha' began to describe a semicircle. The retreat seemed to satisfy the chopper. 'Thank you for your cooperation,' the loudspeaker intoned. 'Have a nice day.'

'Thank *you* for leaving us be,' Cally muttered as the helicopter veered away towards Molohalu. 'And you have a terrible day, y'hear?' Though she continued to act the innocent tourist until even the speck of the heli-copter was no longer visible. 'Okay, let's move.' Brisk now, and purposeful, a Spy High agent in the field. 'Looks like this is as far as you go, Ken. From here on in, it's just me, Eddie and the AquaBikes.'

'Uh, Cally.' Eddie stepped back from the compartment

where they'd stored the bikes, the compartment whose doors he'd already opened. 'I think we've got a problem.'

'What is it?' Cally crossed worriedly to him. 'The bikes?'

'Not exactly.'

The bikes were where they should be, but they were not alone. 'Hi,' said Kiri Ho.

While Eddie and Cally were discovering a stowaway on a fine afternoon in the Pacific, in Littleport, Nova Scotia, darkness had already fallen and Lori and Jake were ready to make the most of it. Shocksuits, shock blasters, sleepshot, they'd packed them all in preparation for a moment like this. Tonight was definitely not going to be a romantic stroll in the moonlight.

'Ready, Jake?'

'Oh, yeah. They don't deserve it, but Rufus Mansfield's Pleasure Cruises are gonna get a second chance of our custom.'

They scarcely needed to sneak, but even though the streets of Littleport were as short of people as ever, like an employer nobody wanted to work for, the Bond Teamers did not allow their vigilance to waver for a moment. They treated the journey to the boathouse as if they were negotiating the Gun Run on maximum difficulty. Somehow, Lori thought, it was the very *quietness* of Littleport that made her nervous. She remembered an old saying her mother sometimes used: quiet as the grave. It didn't make her feel better.

The boathouse, not surprisingly, was in total darkness, the doors stoutly locked. But without an audience this time, that would be no obstacle to entry. The lock was so old-fashioned Jake could pick it without recourse to a deactivator. 'Don't you think the traditional skills are a lot more fulfilling, Lo?' he grinned.

'Let's just get inside,' Lori replied tersely. She didn't trust the Littleport shadows.

Once through the doors she nearly gagged. 'God, Jake, that *smell*.' She had to force herself not to retch.

'I *told* you.' Jake's mouth was twisted in revulsion and he was covering his nose with his hand. 'Salt air and rotting seaweed I *don't* think.'

'What is it, though?' Lori was finding the stench unbearable.

'Who cares? It's the boat we want.' A denser darkness than its surroundings announced the vessel's presence. 'Belt-beams on, but narrow focus. We don't want any inquisitive passers-by to think it's a break-in.'

They pressed the requisite studs on their belts and the hull of Rufus Mansfield's boat could be seen, as weather-worn as its owner, paint peeling like sunburned skin but seaworthy enough, it seemed. Jake investigated further. The cruiser was on the slipway that led to the still-closed harbourside doors. The tide was in tonight. All they had to do was open the doors, release the boat from its moor-ings, start her up and head for Haven Point. At Spy High, they'd learned how to drive, sail or pilot almost anything. After space-spheres and skimmers, this was going to be almost insultingly easy.

'Let's get to work,' Jake said.

They untied the boat so that only inertia kept it from sliding down the slipway. They'd leave the doors until last, when it would be too late for their borrowing of the craft to be stopped. Jake found a ladder and leaned it against the cruiser. 'Hey, Captain Angel,' he hissed into the darkness, 'time to climb aboard and sail away.' Captain Angel did not reply. 'Lori, are you there?'

She was on the far side of the boat from Jake. The stink was worse here, overpowering. It seemed to grow fouler still as Lori approached what appeared to be a trapdoor set into the floor. The reek, the repulsive, suffocating reek of decay. She sensed something lay beneath, something dreadful and noxious that shouldn't be disturbed. The fetid air was almost making her swoon. And though she heard Jake calling her, it was as if the trapdoor was summoning her too. She didn't want to open it. She didn't want to peer down into its dark, disgusting depths.

But she did.

A strangled cry tore from Lori's throat. For a second, she really thought she was going to throw up but if she did she knew she'd never stop.

Bodies. Rotting bodies. Corpses. Packed to the brim. One of them was grinning at her, man or woman it was hard to tell, grinning like a child found out in a game of hide and seek.

Lori was *not* grinning. Her face a grimace of horror, she stepped backwards. Bumped into someone standing behind her. Jake. She really needed Jake's arms around her right now.

She turned to embrace him.

And was eyeball to eyeball with Rufus Mansfield.

'I just couldn't stay behind, Eddie.' Kiri was focussing on him as if he was the weakest link in a chain of disapproval. 'I *had* to be with you. You understand that, don't you?'

'I understand that you disobeyed us,' scowled Ken Ho.

'You want to be a secret agent,' said Cally. 'Sometimes that means accepting orders you don't agree with for the good of the mission.'

Kiri hung her head. Eddie felt quite strongly that he'd like to comfort her.

'Yeah, and sometimes it means breaking orders,' he contributed. 'It means initiative, drive, determination. You've certainly shown those qualities, Kiri, if nothing else.'

'Thanks, Eddie.' She looked up again, smiled.

Eddie faced the vaguely critical expressions of Cally and Ken. '*What?* She's here, isn't she? We can't change that now. Another secret agent thing, Kiri: deal with a situation as it is instead of how you'd like it to be.' He clapped his hands, rubbed them together. 'So, are we getting these AquaBikes ready or what?'

Hauling them out on to the deck and checking their systems did not take long. Neither did changing into the wetsuits that would be necessary for total submersion.

'Eddie,' Kiri whispered in his ear at the last, like she'd been plucking up the courage, 'the saddles on the AquaBikes are quite big, aren't they?'

'One size fits all,' said Eddie, puzzled by the direction of her thinking.

'Big enough for two,' Kiri suggested, 'if the second rider holds on tight to the first.'

'Hold it there.' Cally had overheard. 'If you're angling to come with us, forget it.'

'Why?' Kiri appealed. 'I'm a good swimmer. I know

the 'Aloha' carries spare wetsuits. I won't let go of Eddie.'

The last probably swung it for him. 'Why not, Cal? The bikes *can* carry two and as far as we know this is just going to be reconnaissance.'

'Yeah, and I have problems with the "as far as we know" part.' Cally was aware that she was beginning to sound like a strict maiden aunt. It didn't suit her. 'We don't *know* what we could run into down there. We could be carrying Kiri into unnecessary danger.'

'She's already in unnecessary danger,' Eddie argued. 'I mean, what if Craven's chopper comes back? She's no safer on the boat than she'd be with us.'

Cally sighed. After the ninja attack last night, maybe it *would* be better for her if they kept Kiri close to them. 'Ken, what do you think?'

'It's your call, Cally,' said Ken Ho.

'Okay. *Okay.*' Reconnaissance. That was all they were doing. 'Let's get the bikes into the water. Kiri, if you're not wetsuited up in the time that it takes us you're staying here, understand?'

'Thanks, Cally.'

'Yeah, thanks.' Cally ignored the pat on the back from Eddie. Decision made, at any rate, and once you made a decision in the field, you had to stick with it. She only hoped she wouldn't come to regret it.

By the time the AquaBikes had been pitched into the sea and were bobbing in readiness for departure, Kiri was back on deck.

'Can I ride with you, Eddie?'

The wetsuit kind of *clung* to her. 'You have to ask?' said Eddie.

'We'll keep in contact, Ken,' Cally said, 'and we'll be as quick as we can.' She jumped into the sea and climbed aboard her bike. Eddie followed suit.

'When we get back to land, Kiri,' Ken Ho admonished his daughter, 'you and I need to have a long talk.'

'Of course, Dad.' Kiri kissed him lightly on the cheek. 'See you soon.'

'Full submersible mode,' instructed Cally. 'We don't want them to know we're coming.'

She keyed a command into the control panel. From the fins on the left side of her bike a shield of reinforced transparent plastic curved out, up and over Cally's head, dipping to lock beneath the right side fins, sealing bike and rider in a watertight bubble complete with its own self-sustaining atmosphere. As soon as Kiri was nestled comfortably behind him, Eddie did the same.

'Hold on tight,' he grinned. 'Here we go.'

And the AquaBikes plunged beneath the surface.

Before Lori could cry out, Mansfield's hands, cold, clammy, like Oliver Craven's handshake, were around her throat and squeezing remorselessly.

Then she heard the phut of impact as a sleepshot shell penetrated Mansfield's back. It stopped him. He let her go and she pulled back, choking. Jake was there and Mansfield was tottering.

But he didn't fall. He drew himself erect again. Impossible. Sleepshot was supposed to work on anything organic. Jake fired again. 'Lori. Get out of the way!' Mansfield shrugged the shell off, reached out for her once more, still saying nothing. He seized her shoulders.

The stud in her belt powered up her ShockSuit. Electricity jabbed through Rufus Mansfield but it didn't jolt him into unconsciousness, its traditional effect on assailants. It *deactivated* him. Muscles that were not muscles clenched and froze, like a mechanism that had ceased to operate. Rufus Mansfield still did not fall, but he no longer moved, either. His statue lunge would last for ever.

'Are you okay, Lo? I think he's some kind of animate.'

'I think I've found,' Lori shuddered, 'where the *real* people are.'

Jake looked once, registered the horror, and slammed the trapdoor back down.

'Jake!'

It all seemed so clear now, how the residents of Littleport knew to gather at the boathouse earlier that day in case he and Lori made it inside. How they knew to do the same thing now, to prevent their secret from being communicated to the outside world. Animate bodies. Computer brains. All connected like one big switchboard.

The good citizens of Littleport were thronging at the door, crowding their way inside.

'I think this is our cue to get out of here,' Jake said. 'The boat, Lo.'

But their path was already blocked. By Mrs Carver. By – Jake recognised him with a gasp – the former skipper of the 'Lucky Blue', Captain William Gallagher. And by the other man from the diner, who'd not thought to bring his paper with him tonight. Perhaps he doubted there'd be time for reading.

'Shock blasters.' Jake drew his with a relish that surprised Lori. 'Give 'em everything we've got.'

His first shot shattered one of Mrs Carver's big red hands and left her wrist spouting sparks. His second punched a hole in her midriff. Lori set flames bursting from Captain William Gallagher's mechanical chest. She was glad the animates stayed silent. Even synthesised screams would have haunted her.

Their aim and strike percentage sharpened by two years of training, the Bond Teamers fought their way to the ladder. 'Get on board, Lo.' Jake seemed to have momentarily forgotten that she was team leader. 'Start her up. I'll keep our friends here occupied.'

Lori climbed the ladder. There was no point in disputing leadership right now. Disagreement was a luxury that could not be afforded on missions. On missions, there was always something new to keep you occupied.

Like the controls of Rufus Mansfield's boat. State of the art. High tech. It seemed the owner, and she was betting it wasn't Rufus Mansfield, had been having some work done. Seemed the vessel's true purpose went beyond the occasional pleasure cruise. It was fitted with magnetic propulsion, too. They didn't even need the slipway. 'Jake, come on!' Lori yelled as she brought the boat to life.

'I'm coming!' she heard from behind her. A thud as Jake boarded, thrusting the ladder away from the side. 'And I'm on!'

The animates that could still move were pawing blindly at the hull of the boat. It looked as if they were drowning in a sea of darkness, desperate to be saved. 'No chance,' Jake grunted. 'Blub blub blub.'

'Jake, the doors!' Lori was looking ahead. 'We didn't open the doors.'

Jake adjusted the setting of his shock blaster to Materials, employed the weapon. Major repairs required. 'We did now. Haven Point, here we come.'

EIGHT

It was that dream again, the one he'd suffered seemingly every night since the business with the Temple of the Transformation. The dream that his subconscious seemed determined to send to mock him. He and Uncle Alex, on the cliff-edge again at the Stanton estate, the same scene that had been played out for real a decade ago. Ben looking on while Uncle Alex talked of reaching for the sky, eyes twinkling in the dream with the betrayal that would come, and then throwing himself off the cliff only to rise once more as if walking on air.

But tonight (if it *was* night) the dream was different.

This time it was not Alexander Cain who hovered before Ben's eyes, scaling the sky like a staircase. This time is was Oliver Craven. 'This is interesting,' he was saying. 'Very interesting indeed.'

And then Ben woke up. Sat up. He was in bed but not his own, not at Spy High. He was in a room that could have graced a king's palace, sumptuously decorated in eighteenth century style. Apart from the electricity that was obviously powering the chandelier and bathing the room in light, he could have gone through a time warp.

What was he doing here, wherever here was?

Ben forced himself to think clearly, to remember. The shuttle. The attack. The gas. No residue of it now clogging his mind, confusing him. Whoever had deployed the gas had brought them to this place, probably for interrogation. Capture instead of sudden death usually meant interrogation, which always offered the opportunity to escape and turn the tables. Ben liked to take those opportunities.

'Rise and shine, Bex,' he said. His belt and sleepshot wristbands were gone, and someone had taken the liberty of stripping him down to his boxers (he kind of hoped someone *female*), but modesty did not prevent him from slipping out of bed and padding to the window.

'This is very nice.' Bex observed that she too was in her underwear and as weaponless as her partner. 'What's the view like?'

The courtyards of a pre-Revolutionary French chateau too-many-to-jump floors below, formal gardens beyond, woodland beyond those, and then the land smoothed off and rounded and the ocean, dark in the evening, surrounding all. 'We're on New Atlantis,' Ben deduced.

'Great.' Bex hopped out of bed. 'At least we know who our host is. I kind of hope he's lost the shark, though.'

'Why don't we go ask him?' Ben paced across the room. 'Window's sealed. Let's try the door.'

They opened it. An attractive woman stood in the

corridor facing them. She was smiling. The pair of burly minders behind her were not. 'Oh, no,' she said. 'You can't see Mr Craven dressed like that. Please, there is suitable attire for you in the wardrobe. Cocktails in twenty minutes?'

'How about getting out of here in two?' Bex countered.

The woman laughed artificially. She was probably a lawyer. 'Non-alcoholic cocktails, of course. Twenty minutes. And if you'd like to—'

Ben slammed the door in her face. Courtesy did not extend to captors. 'Wardrobe?'

Bex looked. 'Dinner suit and cocktail dress,' she listed. 'I guess that's for me, though we could *really* confuse them if—'

'I don't think so.' Ben was evidently not in the mood for jokes. *So what was new?* Bex thought. 'We play Craven's game for the moment, and then we change the rules.'

Precisely twenty minutes later there was a polite knock on the door. 'Oh, that's much better,' the woman approved as she regarded the Bond Teamers dressed for dinner. 'Mr Craven *will* be gratified.'

'I'm sorry to hear it,' remarked Bex.

The smile remained fixed, like it was glued in place. 'Please, follow me.'

Oliver Craven was waiting for them several floors down in a gallery hung with paintings and ornate tapestries. A table was set for three to dine, cutlery of gold and goblets of crystal. A string quartet seemed to have taken the wrong turn to the concert hall. Like his reluctant guests, whom the woman rather unnecessarily announced before withdrawing, Craven was formally dressed.

'Ah, welcome, Benjamin. Welcome, Rebecca. Let Phelan fix you a drink.' He gestured to a man with white gloves and a cocktail shaker. Neither Ben nor Bex were thirsty. 'Really? Oh, dear. Well, as I pay him whether he mixes cocktails or not, perhaps I'd better have something myself. Phelan, a martini, please, shaken not stirred.' A knowing aside to the Bond Teamers. 'Or should that be *your* line?'

Ben was evaluating the situation. At either end of the gallery, lackeys were lurking discreetly, or as discreetly as the idiots who worked for creeps like Craven *could* lurk. He decided they'd be hard-pressed to fight their way out of there right now. The ball was still very much in Craven's court.

'I've been looking forward to this moment for a while,' Craven declared.

'Yeah?' Bex snorted. 'That makes one of us.'

'Yes, since I learned about your attempt to interview the late Mrs Bain. By the way, if your little group is still endeavouring to locate Dr Charles Bain, I suggest you call off the search. I'm afraid what remains of him will not be easily discovered. Your companion – Lori, is she called? – may have cheated my hungry pet out of one meal, but I soon put matters right.'

'You killed Mrs Bain?' Ben said.

'Not personally, no,' smiled Craven, 'but I was, you might say, responsible.'

'Good for you.' Ben's tone was acid. 'Just children to go.'

'Indeed.' Craven regarded his audience ruminatively.

'But how do you know who we are?' Bex said. 'And where we've been?'

'Oh, you've been tracked by satellite since your appearance at the Bains' house.' Craven seemed not to think the detail important. 'We watched you taking off in the penal shuttle and what goes up has to come down, as they say. We thought we'd give you a surprise. You needn't worry about the pilots, by the way, if those of you unimaginative enough to stay on the side of law and order do such things. They were deposited safely on the ground, as was their craft. The roof's going to need some work, but still . . .'

'Okay,' Ben's eyes narrowed, 'but you know Lori's name, too.' More than anybody else, Ben didn't like to think of Lori in danger. Old habits died hard. 'How come?'

Craven smiled craftily, like a magician refusing to reveal the secret of a trick. 'I was in Hawaii when my people told me of your little shuttle expedition, concluding some rather important business. Of course, I flew back here directly so I could greet you personally.'

'Shouldn't have bothered,' grunted Bex.

'So I have little news of your *other* friends. The black girl and the annoying red-haired boy.'

'Eddie!' Bex couldn't stop herself. His name burst out like laughter in the sun.

And Cally, Ben thought. Was Craven on to them all? He knew he should have been with Cally.

'Yes. Eddie and Cally, I believe.' Craven shrugged. 'At one point I thought I might need to entertain them as I am the two of you, but then, as I say, the shuttle opportunity arose and I didn't need Cally and *Eddie* – '

spat with fervent dislike – 'any more. Which, I have to tell you, pleased me greatly.' If they'd only known about the Oahu Cup, Ben and Bex would have understood the humiliation and resentment scored in the lines of Craven's scowling face. As it was, they just knew things were looking bad for their friends.

'So what . . .' Ben dreaded to say the words. 'What have you done?'

'Once again,' Craven pointed out, '*I* have done nothing. But my minions, on the other hand . . . What can I say? Don't expect a joyful reunion with Cally and Eddie any time soon.' Oliver Craven checked his watch. 'I'm afraid they'll soon be dead. Shall we dine?'

Beneath the Pacific Ocean, thousands of miles away, Cally, Eddie and Kiri closed in on the island of Molohalu. The AquaBikes' propellers whirred, churning a wake of froth behind them, the machines' fins maintained a perfect balance in the undersea environment, guaranteeing a smooth, fluent ride while, perhaps most importantly of all, the bikes' encircling plastic spheres not only prevented their riders from drowning, but protected them from even getting wet. An AquaBike in submersible mode was like your very own aquarium. The shoals of fish they passed by in flashes of exotic colour did not even seem to think them strange.

Kiri, on the other hand, was entranced by the experience. 'Eddie, this is amazing!' She clutched him close in her excitement. 'I never dreamed that anything like it would be possible. And this is what your life at Deveraux is like *every day*?'

'Nah,' Eddie denied modestly. 'Sometimes we get to do *unusual* things. But listen, Kiri, AquaBikes, all the rest of the hardware we use, they're not ends in themselves. They've got a purpose, you've got to understand that, and the kind of people we're up against, the Cravens of this world, they're dangerous guys, believe me. Being a secret agent isn't just about having fun.'

'No, Eddie, of course not,' Kiri replied dutifully, but her eyes told a different story.

'Eddie, not so fast. This isn't a race.' Cally's voice over the communicator. Eddie had been forging ahead. 'It might be a good idea if we kept together. We're close now.'

'Sure thing, Cal.'

'But you could beat her in a race, couldn't you?' Kiri whispered temptingly in his ear. 'Like you beat Jim Tanner. *I* think you could beat anyone.'

All things considered, Eddie had to agree with her, and it was rare to find someone, particularly of the female persuasion, who appreciated his talents as they ought to be appreciated. Bex didn't. Bex thought he was a loser. So why was he even thinking about her, while Kiri had her arms around him?

Why was he thinking about girls, period? They were supposed to be on a mission. He'd better focus, sharpen up, or he'd be proving the doubters right.

They breasted a ridge in the seabed. The land here began to rise in a pitted, pock-marked but essentially steady slope, the base of the Ninkini volcano. They saw the incline rising further towards the surface, the sunlight, Molohalu.

That wasn't all they saw.

Cally and Eddie both recognised them instantly – the plans of the bombs that Lori had found among Craven's files converted into reality and multiplied. They were ringing the roots of the volcano like a deadly necklace, glittering silver bombcases, their connecting coils stretched tautly like the arms of a man on the rack. Drilled into the rock. The explosives like ugly limpets. Unguarded.

'What the heck?' Eddie frowned. 'Cal?'

'Eddie, what are those things?' Kiri asked.

'You don't want to know,' Eddie muttered.

Cally directed her AquaBike towards them. 'So this is what Craven's been using his Molohalu base for, all nice and secret under water. Planting bombs.'

'Those things are bombs?' Kiri gripped Eddie so tightly he felt his circulation would never be the same again. 'Shouldn't we leave?'

'What, when we've only just got here?' Eddie *kind* of wanted to tell Kiri not to interrupt, but he couldn't quite bring himself to do it.

'There's enough here to make one hell of a bang,' Cally said, riding between the explosive devices and dipping her bike for a closer look.

'But why, Cal? If he detonates this, are they supposed to cause the volcano to erupt or something? Ken said it's dormant, not extinct. Could they do that?'

'They wouldn't need to.' Cally remembered her science. She'd done a course in Natural Catastrophes last year on her own initiative. She'd thought it might come in handy one day. 'If these bombs were all triggered together they'd cause a massive landslide. Maybe the whole of Molohalu would collapse into the sea.'

'So? Downer for anyone on Molohalu but I don't—'

'Downer for anyone living on the Pacific Rim as a whole,' Cally corrected. 'A landslide of that magnitude would generate giant tsunamis that could drown cities and ravage coastlines from the States to Japan. Bye bye, San Francisco. Bye bye, Tokyo. Bye bye, world stability and order.'

'You think that's what Craven's got in mind, Cal?'

'I'm not sure I'm qualified to comment on a twisted mind like Craven's,' said Cally, 'or that I'd want to be, but look at this.'

Eddie steered his AquaBike to join Cally's which was idling above what seemed to be the last in the string of bombs. This one was only partly in place, the main casing fixed to the rock but the drill-tipped cables left to drift in the current like the fronds of some metallic coral, though the holes for them had already been dug.

'So Craven's goons are on their tea break and'll finish up in a minute,' Eddie assumed, 'when *we* shouldn't be here.'

'No, they're not putting them *in*, Eddie.' Cally was emphatic. 'They're taking them *out*. Look along here.' A series of indentations where other bombs must have been set, bombs that were no longer there. 'They're being dismantled.'

'But why?' Eddie didn't understand – not exactly a new condition for him to be in, granted, but frustrating, nonetheless. 'Craven get a better idea?'

'Or a worse one,' Cally mused darkly. 'Either way, I'm betting he came to Molohalu to discontinue this operation. Which begs the question, what's he going to replace it with?'

'E-mail your answer to the Deveraux College, Massachusetts,' said Eddie, 'and be quick about it. Cally, I think tea break's over.'

Advancing towards them on fully submersible AquaBikes of their own, were at least a dozen of Craven's finest. The first torpedo splitting the waters announced that this was not a social visit.

They were well out of sight of Littleport now and therefore able to relax a little. Lori deliberately slowed her breathing, controlled her adrenaline. They'd been taught to master their bodies on missions, not to be betrayed by them. Spy High students could not afford stress, panic attacks or the occasional bout of hyperventilation.

She stood on the deck with Jake while the cruiser's automatic navigator plotted and pursued a course to Haven Point.

'So what did you make of that?' Jake said. 'Nice town, huh?'

'If you like psychopathic animates for neighbours, sure.' Lori tried to maintain a light tone but she didn't feel it. For each of those animates there'd once been a human being, living and breathing, now doing neither beneath the trapdoor of the boathouse and who knew where else besides. 'You reckon the whole place is like that? Nobody normal left at all?'

' 'Fraid not,' said Jake, 'and I reckon it's been that way for a while. Maybe since the sightings of the lights. Maybe that's why they suddenly seemed to stop, because by then the whole town had been, I don't know, taken over. Replaced.'

'But who *built* them?' Lori pressed. 'And why?'

'Good question. The same person or people who installed the system on this crate, that's for sure. And maybe we'll find out when we get to Haven Point.'

Lori sifted possible options. 'There's got to be a Craven connection. It can't be a coincidence that Littleport starts seeing lights and Craven comes to prominence from nowhere at pretty much the same time. I don't believe in coincidence.'

'What does Grant always say? Coincidence is a word invented by the ignorant for a pattern they don't yet understand.'

'A pity at the moment we're lined up with the ignorant,' Lori remarked.

'Not for much longer.' Jake licked his lips in anticipation. 'I'm betting this is Haven Point.'

The sea beneath the boat began to glow, as if a wire had been tripped and a security light activated. It pulsed like a heartbeat, yellow and white, not overtly hostile but eerie, unsettling, casting the cruiser's hull and the Bond Teamers' faces in pale and ghostly colours as they peered over the side.

'So old Gallagher wasn't lying,' Lori said. 'The Littleport lights are real.'

Jake gazed out towards the shoreline. In the night and in the distance it was a denser shade of darkness, nothing more. A headland thrust towards them like an accusing black finger. 'Yep. This is where it all happens.'

'Jake, the lights!'

Lori's nose wrinkled in distaste as a lurid scarlet joined them, as if blood had somehow leaked into the water. The colours expanded, swelled like the petals of weird flowers flung wide to receive the sun, burst like silent submarine fireworks, then gathered again to repeat the process. It was beautiful in its way, almost hypnotic.

'I'm gonna cut the engine,' Jake was informing her. 'Time to start solving some mysteries.'

Lori followed him. 'My communicator still doesn't want to work. Maybe we can contact Spy High from here.' Indicating the array of instrumentation aboard the cruiser.

'Can't. Tried.' Jake seemed engrossed by one display in particular. 'But look at the sonar.' A bead of light flashing, an insistent bleep of sound. 'That's directly below us. Lori, there's something down there.'

The torpedo speared past them, easily evaded, and impacted with the seabed some distance away, pluming up mud and rock and spray. The whole area shook.

'I take it that was a warning shot,' Eddie gritted.

'Stay close to the bombs,' Cally advised. 'They won't fire torpedoes at us here in case they hit them.'

'They sure as heck won't if we hit *them* first. Deploying laser bolts.'

Kiri cried out as Eddie activated the AquaBike's weapons capabilities. Bursts of white fire flashed from the front of the machine, searing scars through the water as targeting systems ruthlessly pinpointed the Bond Teamers' assailants.

The shell of a Craven bike cracked, splintered, water gushing in. Its rider knew the game was up, abandoned his machine and swam desperately for the surface. 'Score one for us!' crowed Eddie.

'One out of twelve's a start, not a finish,' Cally reminded tersely, her own laser bolt capacity boiling the ocean around her. 'They only need to hit two!'

And the attackers were finding their range. Laser fire coruscated by, missing only by inches now as Eddie and Cally manoeuvred with all the suppleness and sudden swerves the AquaBikes would allow. Cally fired in a moment of deadly accuracy and disabled a second Craven machine, sending it spiralling to the seabed like a wounded fish. She shattered the plastic bubble of a third, but as she was trying to elude an attack at the same time, she was forced more and more on the defensive. Eddie was, too, she noted. Maybe it was time to exercise the better part of valour. Spy High had taught them never to be afraid to retreat if no other option was available. A life expended without achievement was a life wasted.

'Let's get out of here!' Cally snapped.

'You're telling me!' Eddie wailed back. 'Inkjets?'

'Inkjets. Full force.'

And suddenly the AquaBikes were bleeding, blackly, copiously. Nozzles protruded along their undercarriage and pumped a liquid the colour of oil into the surrounding sea. It wasn't oil. Its pollution of the pristine waters would only be temporary. But, as the substance expanded to bring a billowing night to the ocean, it would at least provide cover for Eddie and Cally as they sped back to the 'Aloha'.

The Craven bikes might be fully submersible and boast a handy weapons capability, but it was to be hoped that they didn't also possess automatic infra-red guidance systems.

It seemed Eddie and Cally might be in luck. As the inkjets smothered them a few erratic laser bolts still shot by, like lightning in a storm, but soon these disappeared, and as their bikes whooshed away from Molohalu, there seemed to be no active sign of pursuit.

'It's working!' Kiri delighted. 'Eddie, we're escaping.'

'That's the name of the game,' Eddie grinned, the Nelligan swagger increasing with the distance. 'We live to fight another day. More specifically, we live to come back again with *very* big guns.'

'Sonar doesn't detect any moving objects other than ourselves,' Cally recorded from an invisible position somewhere to Eddie's left. 'I think we can lose the inkjets.'

'Whatever you say, Cal.' Eddie turned off the black spray, in seconds racing clear of the cloud behind them. He waved across to his partner. 'Ah, *there* you are.'

'And here's the "Aloha".' Kiri indicated the boat's hull that bobbed above them. 'Dad'll never believe what's happened.'

The AquaBikes rose swiftly to the surface. 'We'd better contact Deveraux, too,' said Eddie. 'Let them know what we've found.'

A rope ladder was already dangling over the side of the 'Aloha' to receive them. Kiri for one, whose smiles of relief quickly faded into a frown, was expecting her father to be waiting on the deck beside it, but Ken Ho was notable only by his absence. Cally and Eddie exchanged suspicious glances as the AquaBikes' spheres retracted and they switched the engines off.

'Maybe you'd better stay here, Kiri,' Eddie suggested. 'Just for a sec.'

'Why?' Frown creasing into something more anxious. 'What's happened? You think something's happened?'

'We just need to check in with your dad. Like now.' Cally was already climbing the ladder.

'Nothing's happened,' Eddie assured his companion. 'Just stay on the bike.'

But he was lying, of course, the kind of lie doctors tell to anguished relatives in hospital waiting rooms. Something *had* happened. He saw what it was as soon as he scaled the side of the boat to join Cally. It was the obvious thing, and irrevocable. He didn't have to look at Ken Ho's body sprawled in an ungainly posture on the deck to know that he was dead.

Cally went to him anyway, an intimate cry of despair in her throat. She knelt, felt for a pulse. It wasn't that Eddie was cold-hearted, but his first instinct was to wonder where whoever had killed Ken Ho had got to.

'Cal!' They emerged from the 'Aloha's' cabin, from the bridge, brandishing weapons and the cruel gloat of the callous.

'Freeze,' warned the first of them, 'unless you want to stop moving for good.'

Eddie stopped obediently, didn't even look round as he heard Kiri's tortured scream from behind him. She *hadn't* stayed on the AquaBike. Maybe she wished she had. 'Dad!' She was running to her father's body, flinging herself down by it, oblivious to the men with guns.

Guns that pointed now not only at the Bond Teamers.

'Leave her alone!' Eddie yelled. 'You don't need her. It's us you want.'

' 'Fraid it's all of you.' The response was icily final. Terminal.

Just as Cally had begun to think that maybe accompanying them had saved Kiri's life after all, seemed she was wrong. All it had done was postpone her death.

PART TWO

ONE

Ben wouldn't allow himself to believe it. Cally and Eddie couldn't be dead. But hadn't they thought the same thing about Jennifer? No. With Jennifer there'd been a body, a funeral, reality. Here and now there was only Oliver Craven's oily word, and Ben wouldn't trust Craven as far as he could throw a SkyBike. This was disinformation, that was all, a trick to confuse them, disorient them. It wasn't going to work.

'The consommé not to your taste, Benjamin?' Craven inquired politely.

'Nothing about this meal or about you is to my taste, Craven,' Ben glared. 'In fact, both make me want to vomit.'

'Oh, please,' Craven simpered. 'How vulgar. But if you must, not on the tablecloth. It's pure silk and scandalously expensive.'

Bex dropped her spoon into her bowl. Consommé splattered the tablecloth, much to her host's disapproval. 'I've kind of lost my appetite, too,' she scowled. 'So why don't we just cut to the chase, Craven? Lying to us about our friends, what's the point of that?' Eddie, she was thinking. After the way she'd treated him, the idea of never seeing him again disturbed her badly, she didn't dare to admit why. 'You think by telling us stories you can frighten us into giving you information?'

'But Rebecca,' Craven chuckled at the accusation, 'I only lie when it benefits me to do so, and at this juncture I can afford the truth. Particularly as I have no need whatsoever to somehow coerce you into supplying me with information. You did that before dinner.'

'What are you talking about?' Bex glanced nervously at Ben.

'Yes, while you were sleeping.' Craven seemed amused that they hadn't realised. 'We took the opportunity to mind-probe the both of you.' The dream, Ben recalled, and Craven's appearance in it. 'Quite extensively, in fact, and what a lot I discovered. The things you youngsters get up to these days! Well, and of course, your little spying organisation. How exciting for you. I'm sure it'll soon be more popular that the Scouts.'

'So if you already know what *we* know,' Ben said, 'why are we still talking?'

'Ah,' said Craven, indicating the table before them, 'I believe in the right of the condemned man – and woman – to be allowed a final, hearty meal before the inevitable.'

'So you're going to kill us?' A wry smile crept across Ben's face. Frankenstein, Nemesis, Talon, Tepesch, even Uncle Alex. Join the queue, Craven, he thought, and prepare for failure.

'I'm afraid your visit to New Atlantis will culminate in a moment of fatality, yes,' Craven admitted almost apologetically, 'but I didn't really like to mention it.'

'Let's change the subject, then,' Ben said. 'As we're obviously not going to be in a fit state to let anybody else know, exactly what were you up to in Hawaii? And why risk drawing attention to yourself by taking over Solartech? Is it the Prometheus Project?'

'Yeah,' Bex joined in. 'Why do you need artificial suns when you're such a natural ray of sunshine yourself?'

Ben triggered a mental stopwatch. Mr Craven, your gloating time starts now.

'Our Hawaiian operation was only ever going to be a diversion,' Craven said. 'A statement of intent, if you like. And as I have instructed it to be discontinued, there seems little point in discussing it further. The Prometheus Project, on the other hand . . .' Craven seemed to grow lyrical, steepling his damp fingers and gazing to the ceiling. 'Prometheus was the man who, according to legend, stole fire from the gods, and now we his successors can light the heavens with suns of our own creation. If we so choose, of course.' Craven sipped knowingly from his goblet and permitted himself a further complacent chuckle.

'Why, what else would you use a man-made sun for?' Ben asked. 'What are you planning, Craven?'

Oliver Craven raised his goblet in salute to the future. 'An event, Benjamin, that you might be grateful you will not live to see.'

'Don't bet on it,' grunted Ben.

'My erstwhile business rival Douglas Elleray had not *quite* grasped the full potential of the Prometheus Project,' Craven continued. 'It took a certain amount of genius to do that.'

'And that's what you consider yourself to be, is it,

Craven?' scorned Bex. 'A genius? Even with all your technology, I think nutcase is a tad more accurate.'

'Oh, I can't take credit for any of this technology, Rebecca,' Craven declared in sudden humility. 'I'm not a scientist.'

'What? But how . . .?' Ben and Bex jointly mystified.

'How? Because I'm not working alone, haven't you guessed yet? What sort of spies are you?' Craven leaned back in his chair, gestured expansively. 'I have allies. Very *special* allies.'

The boat was surprisingly and fortunately well-stocked with oxygen tanks and scuba gear. The suits were a little big for Lori and Jake but fashion tended not to be an issue in the field. They stripped off their ShockSuits swiftly and kitted up ready for the dive. They didn't look away from each other while they changed but they didn't gawp either. Like fashion, romance had little place on operational duties.

'Better keep our weapons,' Jake said. 'Might come in useful.'

'At least until we know what's down there.' Lori fitted her mask and peered over the side at the blossoming bursts of light. 'Jake, we're not going to be in vocal contact from the second we go under. I want us to keep close together. Let me see your eyes. Times like this, it's a good thing we learned sign language.'

Jake's hands shaped an emphatic yes in the air. 'And don't worry, Lo. Nothing is gonna keep us apart.'

'Okay, then.' Lori smiled nervously. 'What are we waiting for?'

In perfect unison they jumped over the side and let the

cold Atlantic waters drag them down. Lori looked up once, at the star-frosted blackness of the night sky, then the sea closed over her head, the only air available was on tap, and around her the strange lights swirled like a shoal of psychedelic fish.

Jake bloomed yellow and red beside her. He was pointing downwards, indicating that they should plunge ever deeper. Lori signalled that she understood. With strong, confident strokes they dived further towards the seabed. No need to even think about their belt-beams: the ocean here at Haven Point was more than sufficiently illuminated to disclose whatever secrets it might hold.

When they saw it, Lori couldn't help but gasp. Her grasp of sign language momentarily slipped from her, but she probably wouldn't have been able to speak either. Jake's eyes seemed magnified behind his perspex mask, unfeasibly wide with astonishment.

Time to start solving some mysteries, he'd said. Score one for Bond Team.

The source of the lights, half-buried in the sediment at the bottom of the sea, was what appeared to be a spacecraft.

TWO

At least they were moving. Being escorted from one part of a captor's complex to another usually provided the best opportunity to bid for freedom, even when guarded. A turn in a corridor here, an open doorway there, tempting resources for a spy with his or her mind on survival. Sadly for them, however, Craven was taking no chances. Minions stuck close on all sides, and already Ben felt certain that they must have passed beneath the ground level of the chateau. It seemed he might have to be satisfied with absorbing all the information about New Atlantis that he could, in the hope that it would be useful later on. In the hope that there would *be* a later on. So, as the seventeenth and eighteenth centuries above were swiftly updated to the twenty-first here below, computers and communications systems, monitoring and maintenance facilities, Ben kept his eyes open and his mouth shut.

Bex was less reticent. 'Aliens?' she whispered in his ear. 'Are we supposed to believe that, Ben? I mean, could it be possible? E.T. with attitude?'

'I can understand your scepticism, Rebecca,' said Oliver Craven, whose hearing was evidently as sharp as his suit. 'All those countless tedious tales of alien abduction. Little green men from Mars, that sort of thing. But my friends are Diluvians, of normal humanoid height, and more blue than green. Ah, here we are. The nerve centre of New Atlantis.'

They'd clearly entered the main control room, and it seemed busy. Scientist types in white coats and old-fashioned spectacles rushed about their work as if they'd heard of a software sale nearby and wanted to get over there quickly. Everything that was portable in the room seemed to be in the process of removal.

'Moving house, Craven?' Bex joked.

'Preparing for what is to come,' Craven replied cryptically.

Several items Ben *didn't* want taken away he spotted in a work-space, presumably awaiting examination. Their belts and sleepshot wrist-bands. Tantalisingly close. Their previous signal to Spy High was now of course obsolete. If he and Bex wanted back-up, they'd need to make contact from here.

'Display the star-charts,' Craven instructed a technician seated before a giant screen that dominated the room. The man obeyed. Ben and Bex had their attention physically directed to the result – the galaxy spread before them. 'Here is Earth, as I'm sure you can tell,' Craven said, 'while here – ' the chart rotated to order, light-years confined to inches – 'is, I am reliably informed, Diluvia, the home planet of my allies.'

'Must go there one day,' remarked Bex. 'It'll make a change from Milwaukee.'

'A planet similar to our own, orbiting a yellow sun,' Craven pursued, 'but different in one major respect. Diluvia is an ocean world, a world almost entirely bereft of dry land, which arrangement has had a most significant effect on the evolution of its people. The Diluvians are amphibious. They are just as much at home breathing water as air. They exist in two environments and are the masters of both.'

'Kind of like fish with legs,' imagined Bex. If Eddie wasn't here, she'd deliver his lines herself.

'You really are quite an amusing individual, are you not, Rebecca?' Craven said. 'I'm sure you'll be missed. But to return to the subject of my allies, they have conquered many worlds over the centuries, preferring those where the ratio of sea to land is more than sixty per cent. Their ability to function in both realms gives them such an advantage, you see.'

'What's the ratio of sea to land on Earth?' Bex asked Ben.

'Seventy per cent of the Earth is covered by oceans,' Ben remembered from Geography text-discs. 'We might as well put an ad in the Galactic Tyrants' Weekly saying come and get us.' Craven was telling the truth now, Ben was sure of it. The code or language on the files that couldn't be translated: Babel chip technology was not yet fluent in Diluvian. The poison that could not be classified: refined on another planet by an alien science. As if Spy High didn't have enough to deal with countering home-grown lunatics.

'So this is what it's all about, is it?' Bex sounded less convinced. 'An invasion from outer space? Is this secretly being filmed by Stevie Spielberg Jr, or somebody?'

'Oh, not an invasion, Rebecca,' said Oliver Craven. 'Not *yet*. An advance party, to pave the way, to weaken Earth's admittedly impressive defences from within, to seek allies who will stand with the Diluvians on their day of inevitable victory.'

'Allies?' Ben coughed. 'You mean traitors, don't you? You mean *you*.'

'You'd side with a gang of intergalactic *fish* against your own people?' Bex shook her head. 'That's low, man.'

'Not fish.' Craven coloured with indignation. 'Amphibians. And what a pity it is that you'll never live to see a Diluvian for yourselves.'

It was like one of those flying saucers from the movies Eddie liked to watch on Twentieth Century Gold. Oval in shape, like an egg, with a far broader disc circling its base, perhaps containing the ship's power source, now half sunk into the sediment. The glistening bluish shell of the craft was not even slightly discoloured by water that would have begun to rust normal vessels – almost as if it belonged here. A sequence of panels girdling the ship close to its highest point pulsed relentlessly in yellow, white and red, the origin of the underwater lights, perhaps a warning, perhaps a threat. Above the disc at intervals there was also a series of sealed apertures which could have marked points of entry into the ship itself. The whole structure was vast, office block high and easily covering the area of a submarine football stadium.

Lori was thinking dates. The first fevered sightings of the lights had been five years ago. Had the ship been here, hidden by the sea, all that time? There wasn't any point in further conjecture on that one. Must have been. But how had it avoided detection as it entered earth's atmosphere? Irrelevant. It evidently had. There was only one question that really mattered right now: was its crew at home?

Two of the apertures, which *were* hatches, slid open, answering that final question. The four figures who emerged from within were plainly not keen on visitors. They were also unlike anything Lori had seen before outside a holoplex. In the form of men, but patently not human. Skin tinged blue as if by prolonged exposure to the cold of deep oceans. Bodies crusted and scaled, apparently devoid of hair. At the head this allowed sight not only of a ridgeless nose, nostrils set flat into the face and flaring, cold crystalline eyes, and a mouth with thin blue lips and jagged teeth, but also the absence of ears, the slits like wounds sliced into the side of the head just above the neck and quivering. The aliens – an unhelpfully general term that would have to suffice for the moment, Lori thought – seemed to have no trouble breathing in water. They were doing so without any visible artificial aid, at least, and they wore only what appeared to be plate armour, like the shell of a crab.

They swam with a strength Lori knew she and Jake could never match, with the power of beings in their natural element. And they had weapons – like an inter-planetary variation on the shock blaster. Lori didn't want to get close enough to be sure.

Jake was staring at her demandingly as the quartet of aliens honed in on them. He was signing a question –

should they shoot? Lori hesitated. What if the aliens were not as hostile as they looked?

They were. Lori flipped to the side to avoid the first burst of fire. She didn't need to give the order now. Shock blasters set to stun, the Bond Teamers fought back. And the aliens might have had an edge given their immediate surroundings, but Lori and Jake were better shots. Two shock blasts. Two casualties. Now the odds were even.

The conscious aliens were fast learners, however. They increased their speed through the water, became blue blurs, zigzagging with such skill that there was no way to target them successfully. Lori found her shock blasts fizzling out harmlessly in the alien's wake. And she was having to evade their assailants' fire too. She doubted that those weapons were on stun.

Lori made the field gesture to Jake that meant they should split up, take one enemy each. Sometimes you had to fight your own battles. Lori thrust higher, towards the surface. Maybe if she reached that . . . but she was never going to make it. She felt the heat of a near-miss through her scuba gear, the alien in pursuit of her grinning at the prospect of a kill. Only one chance for her. If she couldn't hit it by firing directly, maybe she'd just have to anticipate a little, aim at where it was *going* to be rather than where it was. She had no time for another plan. The rubber of her suit was scorched, that last blast was so close. It had better *be* the last. Lori calculated time, distance and trajectory. She fired.

The alien slammed straight into the shock blast.

Jake, meanwhile, had seen none of this. His own foe had in the end spurned the use of weaponry, and adopted a more hands-on approach to his attack. Its hands at that moment were on Jake's windpipe, squeezing. Jake's defences had been breached, the alien had been too quick for shock blaster or sleepshot, and was now too close for either to be deployed. It was all Jake could do to stop his opponent from ripping out his breathing-tube and flooding his lungs with water. The alien was definitely stronger than him but drowning was *not* the way he'd finally hoped to go.

Then the alien's blue-scaled body was juddering like a vehicle suddenly out of fuel. Lidless eyes rolled up into its head so Jake could see the whites, though even these were nearly blue. No problem now to unlock clammy claws from his neck, to let the alien drift restfully to the seabed.

As the body dropped, Lori was revealed behind it, shock blaster in hand. Jake offered her a heartfelt thumbs up.

But relief was only temporary. The mission was still far from over. Lori indicated the spacecraft, the now-closed hatches from which the aliens had issued. Her meaning was clear.

Time to pay a call on the new race in town.

'When do we get to the exit part of the tour, Craven?' Bex wanted to know.

'I'm afraid your little excursion ends here,' the man replied, almost regretfully. To the accompanying lackeys: 'Secure them to the chairs.'

They'd left the control centre and gone back up a level to the mind-probe room. 'Of course, you've been here before,' Craven had chuckled, 'though I'm sure you don't remember.' The probes themselves, black helmets studded with neural stimulators, were suspended above a ring of leather chairs. Only two of them had been required before; only two of them were required now.

And there was still no reasonable prospect of escape.

Ben had little alternative but to allow himself to be pressed into one of the chairs, Bex next to him on his right. 'Funnily enough, I'm regaining my appetite. How about we head back to the gallery? No?' She heard the flip of a switch and metal bands locked tight over her wrists and ankles. 'I guess that's no.'

Their work completed, the lackeys left the room. Only the Bond Teamers and Oliver Craven remained.

'It's best not to struggle, Rebecca,' Craven advised, seeing Bex testing the strength of her bonds. 'You'll only get a nasty flesh burn.'

'That's nothing to what you'll get when our team-mates track you down,' Bex promised darkly.

'Oh, please.' Craven was politely but firmly dismissive. 'If they are as successful as you have been, then I hardly feel that I need lose sleep. Oliver Craven needs to worry about nothing ever again.'

'Talking about yourself in the third person, Olly,' noted Ben. 'First sign of self-delusional megalomania, that is.'

'Ah, you don't understand,' Craven sympathised, 'but then, you wouldn't, would you? Both of you wealthy, privileged. Remember, I *know* your pasts. You can't imagine what it's like to be born poor, to parents fulfilled by tedium and mediocrity, in a backwater town scarcely significant enough to make the map. You can't imagine.' Craven bridled defensively. 'What hope did I have with an impoverished background like that? I was born nobody and would die nobody. What chance was I given to make my name?'

'You could have worked for it, Craven,' Ben said. 'You could have moved away, anything. In life we make our own chances.'

'And I have.' Craven drew himself tall. 'I have. When the Diluvians came, I was ready. I knew what it meant when they appeared in Littleport and started killing. It was the end of mankind's tenure as lords of the Earth and I could either side with the sheep about to be slaughtered or offer myself into the service of those who would inherit this planet and reshape it in their own image. I don't need to tell you the choice I made.'

'What did they pay you?' grunted Ben. 'Thirty pieces of silver?'

Their captor smiled. 'My dreams have come to pass. Oliver Craven is a name emblazoned upon the public consciousness, a name to be reckoned with. And soon it will be even more. The Diluvians have given me my opportunity and I intend to prove to them how much I deserve it. I intend to show them my true worth—'

'Doing a good job of that already,' muttered Bex.

'—by taking it upon myself to eliminate possible threats to their plans. Your friends in Hawaii, for example. Yourselves.'

'Can we get on with it, then?' Ben interrupted. 'Or is the idea to bore us to death? Let me tell you, Craven, I can feel a coma coming on already.'

'It's just such a pity I can't stay and watch,' lamented Craven. 'It would be interesting to see how long your bravado lasts before it breaks down into begging for your inconsequential life. But some pleasures simply have to be denied. I have an appointment at the Fortress. My private jet is primed and prepared and my allies do not like to be kept waiting. And so, farewell.'

In the distance, rumbles like thunder. The room trembled.

'What's that?' Bex said.

'In a sense, it marks the death of Oliver Craven,' the man himself smirked. 'I'm afraid New Atlantis is sinking. A terrorist outrage, striking before a mayday could be sent. Soon New Atlantis will join her namesake at the bottom of the ocean, a foretaste of the future, and the two of you with her. Perhaps you'll even have a chance to learn the difference between fish and amphibians, Rebecca, if you can hold your breath long enough.'

'Why, Craven?' Ben demanded. 'Why sink New Atlantis?'

'She has served her purpose. Oliver Craven, industrialist and inventor, has served *his* purpose also. A new age is upon us, one that will wash over the old as the sea over the land. I have a place in it. You, I am afraid, do not.'

And as Craven departed and the Bond Teamers were left alone, the vessel shook with the ominous boom of further explosions. The mind-probe room seemed already to be tilting.

Bex imagined the cold ocean waters flooding in, their level rising inexorably, lapping at her mouth, her nostrils, drowning her eyes. 'Ah, Ben,' she ventured. 'If we're gonna go, I reckon we should go *now*.'

The deactivator was taking its time. The alien circuitry in the locking mechanism seemed to confuse it. If the device had had a head, it would have been scratching it right now. *Come on, come on*, Lori was pleading silently. The arrival of blue-scaled reinforcements at this point would have she and Jake trapped against the hull of the ship, easy targets. She saw the same fear reflected in Jake's eyes.

But Spy High technology always won through in the end. Suddenly the hatch was sliding open. Whether what lay beyond could justly be called an airlock when it was full of water was an interesting question, though one to consider maybe later in the comfort and security of the rec room. Lori retrieved the deactivator, replaced it in her belt and then, shock blasters ready, she and Jake edged inwards.

No welcoming committee. That was a good sign. Maybe the four unconscious aliens presently littering the seabed were it. Hopefully. But no air, either. The ship was flooded, the water within somehow purer of colour than that of the Atlantic, as if it had been refined. The Bond Teamers swam warily into a corridor which seemed to wind through the craft organically, like it had evolved rather than been manufactured. Everything was curved, rounded, the corridor that Lori and Jake followed was like the blue sweep of an impressionist's brushstroke. The doorways they passed were circular too, no sharp edges or hard corners anywhere.

Lori felt Jake squeezing her arm. He was gesturing to a sealed aperture that appeared larger than the rest, perhaps suggesting that on the other side might lie something of importance. This time the deactivator worked more quickly: maybe it was getting used to the aliens' technology.

Jake's supposition was correct.

The chamber the teenagers now entered had a clear and disturbing purpose. The creation of animates. On the walls were templates of the human form resembling diagrams from an anatomical textbook. Limbs and torsos and heads in regimented rows, as if awaiting inspection, some still at the raw metal alloy stage, others partly or entirely disguised with pink human flesh. The artificial skin was growing in vats around a table where the false body parts would be fixed together to form a parody of life, and where the lie of identity would be completed by an animate-surgeon crafting the face of someone who by now was dead. This was where the present population of Littleport had been born.

Jake's eyes narrowed with disgust. He raised his shock blaster, changed the setting to Materials. Lori's turn to squeeze *his* arm. She signed 'no', then 'evidence'. Jake signed nothing, but his resetting of his blaster to Stun demonstrated acceptance of Lori's point, however grudging. She indicated that they should move on.

The corridor finally opened up into a vast arched chamber that was clearly the hub of the ship. At its centre a flickering dome of instruments and screens and controls announced its own significance, while this was reinforced by the presence of some thirty glass or plastic egg-shaped capsules, man-sized and transparent, set into the circular wall and abundant with tubes and sensors, each banded by some kind of locking mechanism. Cryo-pods, Lori guessed, to preserve the crew of the ship in suspended animation while their craft traversed the timeless expanse of deep space. So they'd be nice and fresh when the time came to start slaughtering innocent Earthmen. All life support systems were probably monitored and maintained from here.

Jake was requiring her attention again. He seemed to be counting for her, three bursts of fingers. Ten. Twenty. Okay, so there were exactly thirty cryo-pods in the chamber. Addition had never been a problem for . . . and then, of course, Lori realised what Jake was saying, and why the number of pods *might* be a problem. Thirty minus four left twenty-six. Over two dozen aliens still unaccounted for.

Make that two dozen precisely.

Bursts of fire from the chamber doorway. Dual sources. Only super-fast reflexes and minds that had been trained always to be alert saved them. On land, Lori and Jake would have dived, rolled, sprung up fighting. Here beneath the sea, however, the water pressure limited their options. They separated, surged across the chamber in a sudden agitation of spray, sought refuge behind the cryo-pods, brought their shock-blasters to bear from there.

Lori kept low, glimpsing the blue scales of the aliens in the doorway. Maybe they'd be reluctant to fire at the intruders now for fear of damaging the cryo-pods and jeopardising a comrade's safe return to whatever planet spawned them. Then she was recoiling as a bolt from one of the alien's weapons struck the pod and shattered it, splinters sharding close to Lori's face. Maybe they didn't plan on leaving.

Or maybe they were just reckless. Lori recovered quickly, ready to defend herself again, but here came the aliens. Their guns were blazing at the Bond Teamers, yes, but they were sacrificing their cover quite needlessly, risking all to reach ... The central control dome. Lori didn't know what they were up to, only that they had to be stopped before they could do it. She fired. Jake fired. Bad news. They'd picked the same target. The blasts sent the alien spinning in the water, sure, but his companion was virtually at the control dome. Shock bolts redirected. Alien fingers working. A soundless cry from an other-worldly throat as the stun blasts struck from both sides, but was it a yell of despair or triumph?

Lori and Jake swam to the control dome. The alien had done something. They hadn't eliminated him quickly enough.

And now they might have to suffer for it.

One of the panels on the dome was flashing green. On Earth, Lori thought, green usually meant good. But given the sudden, grating, siren sound that was reverberating through the ship and that could only be an alarm, perhaps the colour carried a different connotation on the aliens' home planet. Given that the panel featured a display of symbols that she couldn't comprehend but that seemed to be changing every second, Lori had a pretty clear and entirely chilling idea as to why the ship was screaming. What else do you do when you're about to die?

Whoever these aliens were, they evidently took no prisoners. The ship was set to self-destruct.

The floor was certainly tilting now, with all of New Atlantis shivering as if sensing that the dip it was about to take was going to be both cold and permanent.

'So what are you waiting for, then?' Ben reprimanded, craning his neck to the right so he could see Bex more clearly. 'I assume your ring's a product of Spy High and not a cheap gift from Eddie.'

'Right on both counts,' said Bex, though resenting her partner's reference to Eddie when they still didn't know whether he was alive or dead. Tact was not a familiar term to Ben Stanton.

'So what is it? Laser charge? Jamming signal? Knock-out gas?'

'Laser charge.' Bex made a fist of her left hand, looked down at the ring on her index finger, a silver band inlaid with a small stone that could have been a ruby but wasn't. 'But what good is that?' She'd sprung them all from their cell in the Temple of the Transformation's pyramid with a similarly customised navel stud, only then there'd been a control panel to hit. 'What am I gonna fire at?'

'Me,' said Ben.

'Don't tempt me.'

'I mean these manacles. Far as I could tell, they were all operated from the same switch in the back of the chair. No way you can hit the back of the chair, but maybe if the laser can short-circuit even one of the manacles, it'll disengage the others as well. Can you move your wrist enough?'

Bex flexed her forearm. It was lucky Ben was to her left – it was just possible to get a shot in. On such small matters did secret agents' lives depend. 'If I miss, Ben, you're gonna need more than after-sun lotion.'

'I think laser scalding'll be the least of my worries if you miss, Bex,' Ben grunted. 'How about just getting on with it?'

'Whatever you say, former leader-person.'

The shot was actually likely to be the easy part. Energising the ring was going to be harder. Obviously, it wouldn't do much for Spy High's image or, indeed, its continued concealment, if laser rings issued to agents were in danger of going off at awkward and inopportune moments, when the wearer's hand was engaged in otherwise normal social activities, like waving, using cutlery or shaking someone's hand. The ring was not activated therefore by any kind of pressure, but by its jewel being raised and turned a full three-sixty degrees. Simple enough with both hands free, but Bex had neither. The thumb and middle finger of her left hand would have to suffice.

Bex drew back these digits, keeping her index finger extended. The ring was close to her knuckle. She eased it forward a little, flicked up with her thumbnail. The false ruby clicked into active position. Then Bex slowly, gradually, used the ball of her thumb to rotate the stone.

'I don't like to interrupt a girl who's so obviously enjoying her work,' Ben said, 'but unless you get a move on we'll be seeing how effective laser rings can be under water.'

Bex glanced across, not so much at Ben himself as at the position of his manacle. As soon as the ring's revolution was complete, the laser would fire and it had a single charge only. After that, Bex would be reduced to wearing just jewellery.

She twisted her hand to the left as far as she could. Hoped it was far enough. Thumbed at the ring. Heard the click to signify that it was energised.

The laser bolt struck the manacle of Ben's right hand dead in the middle. It sprang open as if in pain. The others copied it simultaneously.

Ben was on his feet just as quickly, flipping the switch on Bex's chair that he'd seen Craven's man use, releasing her. 'Good work,' he acknowledged.

'Why, thank you,' Bex grinned. 'Now about getting out of here . . .?'

No doors were locked and no one was about, neither observation surprising Ben. The need for security was past. New Atlantis was listing badly now. Ben imagined the great air cushions crumpling, the transplanted trees tugging at their shallow roots as the level ground fell away, the antique furniture in the chateau sliding inexorably to one end of each and every exquisite room. He'd lay odds that he and Bex were alone on the sinking structure. And there remained one thing yet to do.

'Ben, where d'you think you're going?' his partner protested. 'Down is drown. Up's the other way. You know: surface, sunshine, survival.'

'Down is the main control room,' Ben reminded her. 'We're probably miles out at sea and sinking like a stone. We need to signal Spy High and we need our belts to do it. Just hope Craven's men haven't taken them with them.'

'Hope's the word,' Bex moaned as she kept pace with Ben. 'I don't fancy having to swim all the way back to the mainland.'

Like all good agents, they'd both memorised the geography of New Atlantis. They headed down a level and right to the control room. Again, the luck was with them. Right was still above water. Turn left and they'd have been wading the final few metres. The ocean was making swift progress through the lower levels of New Atlantis.

'Let's be quick, though, huh, Ben?' Bex suggested, eyeing the water's advance with trepidation.

It looked as if they could be. Their belts and wrist-bands had not been moved. Either the retreating technicians had forgotten them in their haste to depart New Atlantis before it went down, or they'd thought the prisoners' trinkets too inconsequential to bother with. The Bond Teamers seized their equipment gratefully. Buckling her belt on, Bex immediately felt better. A little sun on her back and she might even feel *good*. She pressed the emergency tracer signal on her belt, saw Ben do the same. A Deveraux rescue helicopter would be scrambled within seconds.

'Onwards and upwards?' she urged. Water was trickling into the room.

'Not just yet.' Ben was seating himself at a computer console, activating the screen that had shown the star-charts.

'Ben, and trust me on this one,' Bex said, 'now is not the time to start playing computer games.'

'There's information we need,' Ben justified tersely. 'Where Craven is going. It won't take long.' Then, thrown down like a challenge: 'You can leave if you like. I'll see you up top.'

'Oh, no,' Bex refused. 'What, have the meek and mild girl stand by on the sidelines while the big brave boy hogs all the action? You're not getting rid of me *that* easily, Ben Stanton.' And whose laser ring got us even this far, she might have added, if she hadn't thought doing so would break Ben's concentration. Instead, she watched him work at the keyboard. It looked like Cally had taught him a trick or two.

'Craven said something about having an appointment at a fortress,' Ben said. 'Assuming he's flown directly there from here, his flight plans might be plotted in the computer's memory.'

On the screen appeared the most recent functions the computer had performed – Bex recognised the maps of the galaxy Craven had shown them one after another, like counting backwards or watching a movie in reverse. And finally, 'Gotcha!' Ben triumphed.

The screen showed New Atlantis to be in the Atlantic off the coast of Florida, its position pretty much unchanged from when Jake and Lori had visited. The computer had drawn a line from there heading north, always north, along the eastern seaboard of the United States and then diverting inland across Canada. The flight path came to a bleeping end in the arctic wastes of Canada, about as close to the North Pole as solid land would take you.

'What are Craven and the Diluvians doing up there?' Bex pondered. 'Nothing but snow and ice for company that far north.'

'Well, we know they're not going to be cold,' Ben commented. 'The Prometheus Project'll see to that – plenty of artificial sun.'

'You think that's what they're up to? Building a sun? But what for?'

'Not sure,' mused Ben, 'but I know one thing. Fire and ice don't mix. You put them together and either the fire goes out or the ice . . .' Ben paused. He suddenly had a very clear and very frightening idea as to what the Diluvians intended. 'I think we'd better get back to Spy High as quickly as possible.'

Water was now pouring into the control room 'I'm with you there,' said Bex.

❊

The good thing about a self-destruct program rather than, say, a bomb, Lori comforted herself as she and Jake flitted through the spacecraft's corridor with muscle-aching swiftness, was that the timing mechanism must have been set with a sufficient margin to allow the crew to evacuate the craft *before* it atomised. She hoped. Because the bad thing about a self-destruct program was the same as any other countdown that culminated in an explosion: if you *were* caught in it, you were dead.

They needed the deactivator at the hatch again, which had inconsiderately closed behind them as they'd entered the ship. This time Lori left it there. If they got back to school in one piece, the techs would provide her with another. Retaining all your field equipment was not a priority when you were swimming for your life.

She gave barely a glance to the unconscious aliens on the seabed. Little chance of them waking up now. Instead, Lori urged herself to swim faster, higher. The surface was a mocking, unattainable distance above her. And there were no lights now, she registered, as if the spaceship had drawn in upon itself before its final act of suicide.

How far away did they have to be? What distance was a safe distance?

The explosion sounded behind and below. Lori heard it. Didn't look back. The shockwave would be following. Jake was beside her. She reached for him, for his hand. They couldn't outswim the shockwave. It would either buffet them or break them. Their fingers brushed.

And then the water struck them, liquid with the force and impact of stone. It tore them from each other. It flung them away, battered their muscles, bruised their bones. Lori's breathing tube came loose and she nearly swallowed salt water. She could barely cling to her senses but she had to stay conscious. She had to stay alive, and to stay alive she had to think. Go limp. Ignore the pain, the heat of waters that had boiled at the point of detonation. Ride the shockwave to the surface.

And when you get there, gasping, spluttering, exhausted, your muscles like mush, count your blessings.

It was dark and difficult to make out even Rufus Mansfield's boat a distance away. Lori didn't care about the boat. 'Jake! Jake!' She scanned the sea with desperate eyes. Jake had to have made it as well. He *had* to have done.

'Lori! Lo! Over here!' A black shape bobbing.

And he had. Despite everything, Lori found herself laughing.

Jake swam towards her. 'You okay?'

'I am now.'

Wearily, they returned to the cruiser, clambered aboard. The vessel's navigation systems were all defunct. 'They must have been controlled from the aliens' ship,' Jake said. 'Now that's gone . . .'

'A spaceship.' It was her first chance to actually say the words. 'An *alien* spaceship.' Lori seemed to want to make the most of it. 'Water-breathers.'

'Yeah,' Jake frowned, 'and still plenty of them at large if those cryo-pods are anything to go by. If only we could . . . hey, wait a minute.' An idea had occurred to him. Jake fiddled with his belt communicator. 'We're online again. The aliens must have been sending out some sort of jamming signal.'

'Grant won't *believe* what's been going on,' predicted

Lori as their Senior Tutor took the call. But Grant *did* believe what had been going on — his training had included the unlikeliest of scenarios — but only just. 'We'll get people to Littleport as soon as we can,' he promised.

'I don't think we're going to need to worry about the aliens' animates any more, sir,' said Jake. 'I'm betting they were controlled from the ship as well.'

'Sir?' Lori ventured cautiously. 'What about the others?'

The pause over the communicator was enough to chill Lori's heart. When they came, Grant's words only confirmed the worst. 'Lori, Jake, I'm afraid there's some bad news . . .'

THREE

They were told the details during a muted, despondent debrief. Found: the wreckage of the 'Aloha'. Found: the floating corpse of Deveraux Selector Agent Ken Ho. Found: the remains of a hastily disbanded Craven operation on the island of Molohalu. Missing: Ken Ho's teenaged daughter, Kiri. And missing, most significantly for the four members of Bond Team now returned to Spy High: graduate agents Eddie Nelligan and Cally Cross. No evidence. No bodies. No trace.

'That's good, isn't it?' Bex was trying to convince herself as much as anyone else. 'I mean, isn't that good? It means they could still be alive somewhere. Captured or something.'

'That's right,' Jake concurred. 'Just not in a position to contact school. Until we know otherwise for *sure* . . .'

'Let's hope so,' said Lori.

Ben said nothing. He was thinking about the teaming of Cally with Eddie. He wouldn't be so insensitive as to mention this to anyone else, least of all Lori, but he couldn't help feeling that if Cally had been paired with *him*, she wouldn't be missing now.

Senior Tutor Grant sent them to the recovery suite. Ben and Bex, having spent time as the beneficiaries of Craven's hospitality, were first probed and screened for implants of any kind, for chemical substances added to the blood. Once declared bug-free, they joined their team-mates in the nutrient baths, immersing themselves in a solution designed to accelerate the healing of bodies damaged in the call of duty.

If Eddie had been here, Bex thought, he'd have been asking for the soap or trying some dumb line, and she'd have snorted at him and told him to get lost or grow up or get a life. Right now she wished she had a chance to do that. Spy High seemed awfully quiet without Eddie, like a party when the guests have gone. She'd been too harsh on him before, too cruel. If she could change the past, Bex would, but not even the technology of the Deveraux College extended to altering timelines.

Ben, feeling his skin soothed and invigorated by the nutrient bath, was in the realm of what-might-have-beens. With Cally. There'd been the potential for something between them, hadn't there, the possibility of a relationship, however unlikely? Social opposites, like black and white. Ben was thinking he'd have liked a chance to make it work. He wondered what it would have been like to be with her, what she'd say in secret moments, what she'd do. But there was still a chance. He had to hold on to that, they all did. Bond Teamers were hard to kill.

After the baths, they were fitted with sensitiser helmets: tranquil sounds for the ear, fragrant odours for the nose, and a kaleidoscope of gentle, calming colours before the eye. But none of them worked to de-stress Lori. She didn't see the peaceful greens and blues and whites. Her vision was filled with images of Eddie and Cally, her mind with fear of their fate. And worse, no number of sensitiser helmets or nutrient baths could assuage her guilt. She could think of only one way to do that.

'I'm resigning,' she said.

'What?' They were in the girls' room and Jake expressed the common astonishment.

'I'm going to see Grant to resign from leadership of Bond Team. Right now.' Lori stood to prove her point.

'No way.' Jake was on his feet too, blocking his girl-friend's path.

'Excuse me, Jake. You're in my way.'

'You bet I am, and I'm not getting out of it all the while you're talking like this.'

'Jake's right,' said Ben, a 'for once' left hanging in the air. 'It's not your fault what's happened – what might have happened. Resigning because you're upset doesn't make any sense. We're *all* affected.'

'I know that,' retorted Lori, 'but we didn't *all* select the teams. Only I did that. It's my fault Eddie and Cally were sent to Hawaii so it's my fault they haven't come back.'

'*Yet*,' reminded Bex. 'Haven't come back *yet*. And I don't really follow the logic of what you're saying, Lo.'

'Team leadership brings with it responsibility, sure,' Ben spoke from experience. 'But that doesn't make you to blame for everything that goes wrong. Eddie and Cal have had the same training as us. They know the risks.

We're responsible for our own survival in the field, Lo, and you weren't even *in* Hawaii.'

Lori seemed swayed. 'But – I don't know – I've got to do *something*.'

'A dramatic gesture that won't change anything isn't it,' Ben asserted. And then he said something that the Ben Stanton of last year would never have been able to say. 'And we still trust you, Lo. We all want you to stay as our leader, don't we?'

'Absolutely,' said Bex emphatically.

'Ditto,' nodded Jake, 'and I'll tell you what we do as well. We wait until Grant locates this fortress for us – Craven, the Diluvians, the whole sick crew – and then we take them out. We do now what we did when we lost Jennifer. We take revenge.'

Out of the frying pan and into the fire. In Spy High terms, out of a boat bulging with psychopaths pointing guns and into a helicopter bulging with psychopaths pointing guns. If he ever did make it as far as the next stage – out of the fire and into a nice comfortable bed or something – Eddie imagined he'd be suffering from staring down the barrel of a pulse rifle withdrawal symptoms. Craven's men seemed keen not to let him, Cally and Kiri out of their sight, or, indeed, out of their sights. And one last thing about the frying pan and the fire as well, Eddie shivered, at least both were a tad warmer than the bitter, biting air outside the chopper as the snowbound Canadian forests passed by beneath them. Their captors had been good enough to let them change back out of their wetsuits, but their generosity had not extended as far as thermals. Nor, indeed, to letting them keep anything that remotely resembled a weapon or a signalling device.

But Eddie wasn't really worried about his clothing or himself. He was worried about Kiri. She was huddling against him now and shaking almost uncontrollably, eyes wide and staring with disbelief and denial. Like a frightened animal. Like a rabbit in a snare. Maybe Kiri Ho wasn't as fit for secret agent work as she'd declared herself to be, Eddie thought, and then hated himself for it. He hadn't just seen his father murdered.

'Try and hold on, Kiri,' he whispered to her, squeezing her in what he hoped was a comforting way. 'Stay cool. Keep it together. Wherever they're taking us, we need to be ready.'

And it was the where that was interesting Cally. Obviously not New Atlantis or any Craven Industries location that the files knew about. Of course, there was a lot about Craven Industries and its CEO that the files *didn't* know, a lot that was kept under the surface, so to speak. But out here, in the trackless wastes of the Canadian North, the arctic circle, what could possibly be awaiting them? There was nothing as far as she could see but gulfs and cliffs and ravines of ice, the terrain too frozen now even for the hardiest of trees to flourish. A white plain in all directions, so white it was almost blue, frosted to the sky and dazzlingly painful to the eye. The ice from here, Cally guessed, might stretch the entire distance to the pole without interruption.

Only it didn't. She was squinting but she was sure. Something was jutting from the snows ahead of them. 'Eddie!' she hissed. 'Heads up!'

At first sight it looked like a glacier of mountainous

magnitude. It looked like a sheer and shimmering block of ice that could not be scaled or passed. But as the helicopter drew nearer, dropped in altitude towards it, Cally could see that there was nothing natural about this edifice in the arctic. What had seemed a colossal ridge rearing from the rock was in reality a massive, seemingly impregnable wall, metal camouflaged white to blend with its environment. The chopper was descending towards some kind of fortress, towering and titanic, essentially square in shape and, as they hovered above its roof, totally sealed from prying eyes but for a single translucent dome in its centre, like the film across a frozen lake. Within it Cally glimpsed an orange glow like the coals of a distant fire. She craned her neck for a better view but the roof also featured a heli-pad and their transport was making smartly for it. 'Guess we're here,' she said.

'Thanks for the lift, guys,' Eddie said cheerfully as he, Kiri and Cally were bundled onto the roof. 'Sorry about your tip, but I left my wallet in my other trousers.' Kiri slipped on the icy surface. Eddie held her, whispered in her ear. 'Stay close to me. Do whatever I tell you to, okay? Kiri?'

She looked at him dumbfounded, nodded, but Eddie could tell that it wasn't okay. It wasn't okay at all.

Pulse rifles prodding at their backs prevented further talk and encouraged all three prisoners towards a hatch that had opened, providing access to the stronghold. 'Let's hope it's a bit warmer inside than out,' muttered Eddie.

The interior was more or less familiar to the Bond Teamers, a variation on a theme established by would-be world conquerors and assorted madmen from Stromfeld to Alexander Cain: corridors, computers, and uniformed guards with guns. Plenty of guards with guns. Eddie felt that he could cope. They'd practised countless escape from the villain's lair scenarios during their time at Spy High. It was all new to Kiri, however, strange and intimidating.

'Eddie, where are they taking us?' she said in a voice that was unsettlingly close to a whimper. 'What are they going to do to us?'

'We'll be fine, Kiri,' Eddie calmed. 'Remember what I said. Be strong.' But he exchanged a worried glance with Cally. Whatever move they made, they had to consider their companion. Kiri Ho was their responsibility.

They were met by a guard who took charge with the ease of habit.

'Someone in authority at last,' Eddie said. 'So where do we go to check in?'

The man's eyes glittered. 'Checking in suggests the possibility of checking out again,' he observed. 'The Commander wants to see you.'

'Commander? Craven given himself a new title now? He's never happy, is he?'

No response from the guard but a knowing half-smile.

'Does the tour come with an audio commentary or does that cost extra?' Eddie quipped as they were led towards what his sense of direction told him was the core of the base, its heart. It *was* warmer here. Considerably so.

And in a chamber of computer consoles, with technicians scurrying about their business like drones, a figure stood with his back to them as they entered – a tall figure, imperious. But bald? Eddie registered. And *blue*?

And kind of scaly . . . And what had happened to the guy's ears? No way was this Oliver Craven.

Yet the guard was announcing, 'Commander, the prisoners.'

And the commander was turning to regard them with cold expressionless eyes. When he spoke, it was in an accent that Eddie instinctively knew was not of this world.

'Welcome to the Fortress,' he said, as a hangman might greet his victim on the gallows. 'My name is Commander Krynor.'

The final preparatory briefing was almost over and that suited Jake Daly just fine. He didn't want to be stuck in Briefing Room One with his team-mates, Grant, Corporal Keene and a variety of tight-lipped, stiff-backed military types. He wanted to be out there, speeding towards Craven and the Diluvians, shock blaster in hand and primed to do some damage. For Eddie. For Cal.

'But remember – ' maybe Grant had joined psi-division in his spare time and was now reading minds – 'we need to keep cool heads throughout this whole operation. Not one of us can afford to let what may or may not have happened to Agents Nelligan and Cross affect our conduct in the field. Personal feelings stay here. When we finally confront the Diluvians, I want only cold, considered action.'

'Let's get on with it, then,' muttered Jake, earning a scolding glance from Lori.

'With the information provided by Bond Team,' Grant continued, 'we've been able to make progress in several areas. The techs have been working hard to upgrade our Babel technology so that the Diluvian language can be translated, so we'll at least know what the aliens are saying. And our sentry satellites have detected some anomalous electrical activity in northern Canada around the area to which Oliver Craven seems to have fled. Visually there's nothing, but the techs have analysed the anomaly and found it to be consistent with a small-scale distortion field, keeping this so-called Fortress hidden from our eyes. But it's there. It has to be. And that's where we're going.'

Excellent. Jake was champing at the bit.

'The Diluvians could pose the greatest threat to Earth's security that we have so far faced. No chances will be taken.' Grant regarded the room's occupants levelly, unblinkingly. 'If necessary, we will eradicate this Fortress utterly. And everyone inside it.'

It was probably optimistic to say that Kiri was recovering, but at least she didn't seem to be getting any worse. Maybe sitting in a cell with Cally and Eddie had given her a chance to regain some equilibrium. Certainly her eyes had lost that haunted, hunted look. They were narrowed now, determined, but still they were not so much seeing her immediate surroundings as the body of her father.

'He was a wonderful man.' In hushed tones, like a speech at a funeral. 'A wonderful father. He raised me on his own since Mum died. He did everything for me, loved me, made me feel special. He always said that one day he and Mum would be reunited. I hope that's true. I really hope that's true.'

'We liked him, didn't we, Ed?' Cally was holding Kiri's hands. 'I know we'd only just met him, but he was a good man, we could tell that. We were lucky to have met him.'

'Thanks,' said Kiri, 'but, you know, it's not really fair of me because Dad was a Selector anyway, and that was his choice, but I can't help wishing you'd *never* met him. Or me. If you'd never come to Oahu, Dad would still be alive.'

The implacable logic of grief. Cally looked to Eddie with some embarrassment, even guilt. Was Kiri right? Were they to blame for the girl's bereavement? When they were off on their world-saving missions, did they ever even give a passing thought to the innocent bystanders who might be caught in the crossfire between Good and Evil?

Further consideration of the matter was avoided for the present, however, by the sliding open of the cell door. The three prisoners snapped to their feet. Commander Krynor and several other Diluvians had come to the cell. They'd brought weapons with them, similar to shock blasters, and all were garbed in crustaceous body armour.

'I must apologise for having neglected you,' said Krynor. 'On my planet hospitality to guests, even unin-vited ones, is a matter of honour.'

Eddie switched automatically to wise-cracking mode. 'So can we take it that executing them is entirely out of the question?'

'Sadly for you,' Krynor smiled thinly, 'we are not on my planet.'

'Well, if you get that homesick kind of feeling, Krynor, don't let us stop you from leaving.'

'Exactly why *are* you on Earth, Krynor?' Cally demanded. 'It's obviously not to help establish inter-galactic peace and harmony. How did Craven ever contact you?'

One or two of the Diluvians chuckled at that, per-plexing Cally and Eddie. Commander Krynor's own smile became, if that was possible, even thinner, tighter, an expression of anorexic amusement. 'An old friend of yours has just arrived,' he said. 'I think you should see him. And on the way, perhaps I will show you something of our purpose. Come.'

So Craven was here now, too. The 'old friend' had to be him. Cally felt that quickening of her pulse that she'd come to recognise as her very own biological early warning system of a mission's impending climax. In short, it was all about to hit the fan.

'I guess you Diluvian guys have been busy,' Eddie observed as they were marched through the complex. 'Settling in here. Making this place nice and homely. Learning English. I mean, that took *me* a while and I'm local. But you could have picked a better place to build, mind. You don't exactly get people flocking to the arctic.'

'Precisely the point, boy,' said Krynor. 'We thought it best not to signal our presence to your population before certain preparations had been made. Subsequent devel-opments have proven our choice of location to be most convenient.'

'Convenient for what?' Cally said.

The thin smile became a scar. 'Please,' Krynor directed. 'Through here.'

They entered what seemed to be a silo, vast, circular, and many storeys high. A fierce heat hit them like a solid force. They were standing on a platform that ringed the silo's hollow core. Gazing up, Cally saw the transparent dome that mushroomed from the base's roof. Gazing down, she saw the fire that she had glimpsed from above. Flames seethed and swelled and crashed against the walls like the waters of a blazing sea, restless, turbulent, the breath of a captive dragon yearning to be free. And all that was protecting her or any of the others from toppling from the platform and plummeting to a burning death was a thin plastiglass alloy shield. There wasn't even a guard-rail. Now was not a good time to develop problems with your balance, Eddie judged.

'The Diluvian Empire extends its gratitude to the genius of Douglas Neil Elleray,' Krynor said, not without irony. 'Perhaps we should bestow a minor title upon his widow. Here, children, you see the fruits of the Prometheus Project. Here you are witnessing the birth of an artificial sun.'

Cally may not have been up to scratch on the Prometheus Project, but the artificial sun part certainly required no further explanation. Except maybe what it was for.

'That's real nice,' Eddie applauded. 'Throw in some palm trees and a beach and you've got yourself something going here, Krynor.'

'Eddie,' Kiri whispered, looking at the guns and thinking of her father, 'don't annoy them.'

'Solar technology is a science in its infancy on Diluvia,' admitted Krynor. 'In our submarine kingdoms, perhaps that is understandable. But since we have been on Earth, we are beginning to appreciate its potential, its value for war.'

'War?'

'Indeed, boy. War. Your planet is about to become the latest conquest of the invincible Diluvian Empire. Our fleet is even now gathering in deep space, waiting only for the signal that we have paved the way for invasion.'

'How are you going to do that?' Eddie ventured. 'Pave the way, I mean. Not signal.'

'We are going to turn your world to water,' Krynor said with relish. 'We will recreate our own beloved Diluvia here among you. We will flood your lands, submerge your cities, send your panic-stricken people swimming like plankton to what they imagine will be the safety of your mountain ranges. But no place on Earth will be safe from our armies. We will rise from your seas, breathing your pestilential air when we need to, march to whatever pitiful defences your survivors might muster and destroy them. Scour the mud clean of humankind – except perhaps for a few whom we might enslave or who amuse us.'

'You want to hear a joke?' Eddie gave a sickly smile. 'I'm good with jokes. I can do magic tricks as well.'

'The operation you chanced upon in Hawaii,' Krynor said. 'That was part of our original plan.'

'So you *were* going to cause a marine landslide,' Cally deduced, 'send tsunamis crashing to the coasts, maybe even make Ninkini erupt again. But what stopped you? You were already dismantling the bombs when we got there.'

'When my father was killed,' Kiri interjected coldly, like she had it in mind to do something about it.

Krynor ignored her. It half-occurred to him simply to have her shot – she was clearly not the same as the other two children – but he was enjoying himself too much to order her death now. Perhaps later. 'The Hawaiian operation would have been significant,' he explained, 'but not decisive, and perhaps it would have alerted your authorities to our presence too soon. That is why you are still alive, why we brought you here. The security organisation for which you evidently work is presently unknown to us. That needs to change.'

'If you're looking for information you'd better invest in spectacles,' said Cally. 'Or given your lack of a nose, maybe contacts.'

'Oh,' Krynor replied modestly, 'we have ways of making you talk. No, the Prometheus Project has superseded all other priorities. It will enable us in one dramatic, cataclysmic action to bring annihilation to your world.'

'Fire and ice,' Cally realised, growing cold herself even in the silo's heat. 'You're going to use your artificial sun to melt the ice-cap.'

'Very good, young one,' Krynor approved. 'You have a mind almost worthy of a Diluvian. Soon our sun like a missile of fire will be launched. Combined with the power of our explosives it will blast and burn its way through your fragile pole, melting countless millions of tons of ice, in time deluging your Earth.' Krynor appeared almost to quiver in anticipation. 'And that time is upon you now. A new sun is ready to rise. The day of the Diluvians is dawning.'

'Sir?' one of Krynor's companions ventured. 'Craven?'

'Of course.' The commander seemed to remember himself. 'Craven.'

Oliver Craven was waiting in the control room where they'd first met Krynor. The immediate expression on his face as they entered, a kind of puzzlement mingled with shock, betrayed the fact that he had not expected to encounter Cally, Eddie or even Kiri Ho again.

'Surprise,' said Eddie. 'Did you miss us?'

'Krynor, what is this?' Craven's fingers fluttered nervously. 'What are they doing here?'

'That's right,' Krynor said thoughtfully, 'because you gave orders for the three of them to be killed, didn't you? Orders that had not been approved by the Commander of the Advance Guard of the Diluvian Empire, namely myself.'

Craven smiled weakly. 'But they might have posed a threat to us, Krynor.'

'Us?' With contempt. The Bond Teamers were beginning to learn something of the true nature of the relationship between Oliver Craven and the Diluvian force, where the power really resided.

'But I did what I thought you'd want me to do, Krynor.' Craven was close to blustering. 'I wanted to prove my loyalty to the Diluvian cause.'

'Loyalty is proven by obedience, little man,' replied Krynor tersely. 'Fortunately, some of your subordinates have already learned that. One of them contacted us from Molohalu in time for these interfering children to be saved for interrogation.'

'But they don't know anything,' Craven claimed, 'nothing that can endanger our . . . your plan.'

'As their comrades knew nothing?' Eddie and Cally exchanged startled glances. 'We also hear that you saw fit to carry out a mind-probe under your own authority, and then had the young ones drowned with New Atlantis.'

'*What?*' Cally couldn't help crying out. 'What have you — ?'

'Silence!' Krynor commanded.

Cally bit her lip. There was no value in jeopardising her, Eddie and Kiri's lives now. But what were Krynor and Craven saying? Their team-mates were drowned? All of them? Some of them? No. *None* of them. Whatever the opposition *thought* had happened, Cally had faith that Ben and Bex, Lori and Jake would have escaped, would have survived. She and Eddie were going to follow suit.

'And you, Craven, you presume too much.' Krynor's nostrils flared in his anger. 'You act as if you are in control of your destiny, as if your life and your decisions have meaning. As if,' and here Krynor sneered in derision, his fellow Diluvians echoing, 'you are not a worthless scrap of human scum plucked from obscurity to serve our great purpose for as long as we see fit, but a being capable of equality with the Diluvian race.'

'No.' Automatically, Craven was backing away. His damp palms were raised as if in surrender. 'I didn't mean anything. I didn't mean any offence. I only want to help you.'

'Perhaps it would help *you*, Craven, to be reminded of your place.'

Before any such reminder could be administered, however, a human tech broke in with some urgency from the radar screen he was monitoring. 'Commander!' he cried. 'Multiple signals! Multiple aircraft approaching from the south!'

Krynor was at his side instantly. 'Switch to visual.'

The tech obeyed and the room was suddenly invaded by military aircraft and helicopter gunships streaking in attack formation across the arctic sky, and closing in on the Diluvian Fortress. Eddie could scarcely resist smiling; neither could Cally. It looked like the human scum were fighting back.

'So,' Krynor growled, 'you cannot even be trusted to eliminate our enemies, Craven.'

'But,' Craven would have backed all the way out of the room by now had an annoyingly solid computer console not prevented him, 'this has nothing to do with me. How can it?'

'Did you see your captives perish with New Atlantis?'

'Well, no, not physically, but . . .'

'Then they did not,' stated Krynor. 'Signal the alarm. All personnel to defence positions. Prepare to repel attacks.'

That was the good news, Cally thought. Maybe Ben was on one of those choppers swooping into battle. The others, too, of course. But the bad news was that with his base besieged, Krynor might no longer see a purpose in keeping his prisoners alive. They'd better think about breaking out themselves. At least for the moment, though, the Diluvian Commander was distracted by Oliver Craven.

'You failed us, Craven.' He was advancing upon the cringing unfortunate. 'Abjectly. Miserably.'

'No. I'm sorry. I beg you.' Oliver Craven, CEO of Craven Industries, industrialist and inventor, grovelled for his life. 'I'll do better. I can do better. Please. Don't kill me.'

'I'm not going to kill you, Craven,' soothed Krynor.

Craven sobbed out with the relief of the reprieved. 'Konar here is.'

And Konar here did. A single shot was all it took. There was a splash of red on the shiny computer console and Oliver Craven's body, his glazing eyes disappointed at their sudden lack of sight, slithered to the floor like a broken puppet.

And Konar's weapon was now trained on Cally. This was it. She couldn't just stand and —

'Take them away,' ordered Krynor, his mind as well as his eyes occupied with the airborne forces ranged against him. 'And begin preparations towards the final countdown for launching our sun. Then it will matter little what happens here. Nothing will stand in our way.'

FOUR

Jake watched with envy as the airforce planes and helicopter gunships launched the first assault on the Diluvian Fortress. Streaks of flame lit up the icy sky as missiles seared towards obstinate steel walls. Gunfire, metronomic and mechanised, strafed the gargantuan square stronghold like deadly rainfall. The pilots of the warplanes swooping low over hostile territory to carry out their runs and then banking wildly, madly to repeat the process. The choppers weaving like wasps, not only unleashing their own weaponry on the Diluvians but repelling and avoiding enemy fire at the same time. Because the fortress was not simply enduring the attack like a saint under torture: gunports had opened in its walls. Anti-aircraft emplacements rose like turrets from the roof. The fortress shrilled its defiance as missiles of its own screamed towards their targets.

And Jake was wishing he was one of those pilots in the line of fire. Their lives were in danger, yes, but their task was simple, straightforward. Kill the enemy before the enemy killed you. And they were getting *on* with it. They were making their mark as surely as the black scars on the fortress proved the missiles had found their range. Jake was growing restless with inactivity, losing patience with planning and delay. He wanted to be in the thick of the action too, blowing something up, confronting the Bad Guys face to face, man to alien. They were all the same, the lunatics, the murderers. CHAOS who had brought down the dome on the heads of his family, Talon the scumbag who'd taken Jennifer from him, and now these Diluvians, thinking big and looking to conquer the world. The same. Different faces, different names, maybe, but the same sick and twisted hearts, the same poisonous minds. Well, there had to be an end to it. The madmen had to pay. And Jake was burning to settle their account.

Yet here he was, stranded outside the range of battle with his team-mates and Senior Tutor Grant, twiddling his thumbs aboard a Deveraux spycopter while others did the job he thought he'd been trained for. 'Something wrong, Jake?' Lori looked at him with concern.

Plenty, he thought. 'No,' he said. 'I just don't like being a spectator, that's all.'

'I know what you mean,' Ben agreed, viewing the attack on a monitor screen. 'If you're not in the game, you don't get the glory.'

'So what are we doing here?' Bex moaned. 'We could have stayed back at Spy High if all we were going to do was look at screens.'

'Very important screens, Bex.' Senior Tutor Grant approached Bond Team. He'd heard their complaints and he understood them. If he was their age, he'd be the same. Patience was a skill that came to be valued only with experience. 'The spycopter's work could be crucial to the outcome of the mission and what we learn now might have a material impact on your role in it.'

Grant indicated the multiplicity of monitors, computers, sensors and scanners that surrounded them, the techs translating raw data into information that could be used against the Diluvians. If somebody didn't already know that they were on board a helicopter, they'd have been hard-pressed to guess. The spycopter's main body was sealed from the outside world and entirely self-contained. Its function was to analyse and interpret every aspect of the object, area or installation that it was directed to observe, to diagnose and identify strengths and weaknesses. Knowledge was power, and in the espionage business, knowledge was often also what kept you alive.

Grant might have expanded on that point to his students had an agitated tech not at the same moment intervened. 'Sir! Mr Grant, sir. You'd better take a look at this.'

The urgency in his voice struck Bond Team, too. They clustered around the tech's console, even Jake. 'Well, Channing?' said Grant.

'Heat signatures, sir,' the tech responded. On the screen in front of Channing, an image of the Diluvian Fortress suddenly lost its walls. The spycopter's instruments had already established its interior layout, the number of rooms, the number of floors. Channing used his mouse to guide Grant and the Bond Teamers towards the structure's core. En route they passed a number of orange pulses and a far fewer number in blue. 'The orange signifies humans,' he informed, 'and the blue our Diluvian friends.'

'No friends of ours,' grunted Jake.

'It seems Diluvian physiology is rather different from our own,' Channing observed. 'Their body temperature is lower than ours, for a start. As you can see, there aren't many Diluvians in the fortress – two dozen, in fact, all grouped at strategic points of defence. But that's not immediately what I think you need to see, sir. *This* is.'

The fortress' floor plan rotated ninety degrees. Channing's audience suddenly found themselves falling down a kind of tube towards a heat signature so tremendous that not only could it not have been generated by anything either human or Diluvian but it could also barely be looked at directly, its brightness was so glaring and intense.

'I think,' said Channing, 'we've located the outcome of the Prometheus Project. An artificial sun.'

'How stable?' Grant demanded.

'Not very. In fact, fluctuations in the sun's heat signature suggest significant volatility.'

'What if one of our missiles hits it?'

The tech looked grim. 'It could toast everything from here to the equator.'

Grant considered for less than a second. Patience was good, yes. So was decisiveness. 'Call off the attack!' he snapped. 'Immediate cessation of hostilities. All aircraft to return to primary positions outside the range of the fortress' weapons systems. Await further orders.' He turned to Bond Team. 'See what I mean

about the spycopter? Looks like it's given you something to do after all.'

'What do you mean, sir?' said Lori.

'Isn't it obvious? You're going in.'

'We're getting out,' hissed Eddie.

'Sounds good, Ed,' Cally whispered back. 'Any ideas
as to how?'

Konar and several of his Diluvian comrades formed
a tight knot around the Bond Teamers and Kiri. They
were not exactly loitering on their return to the cells,
either, partly because of the sounds of battle that
reached them even in the heart of the fortress. The
situation, Cally thought, was not one naturally conducive
to escape.

'I hope this thing was built to last,' Eddie observed to
Konar. 'Roof looks a bit shaky to me, what with the odd
bomb dropping on it and all.'

'Don't let it concern you, human. The fortress is a
product of Diluvian engineering. It will be standing long
after you have been forgotten.'

Maybe Konar was as confident as he sounded. Maybe
not. It was the maybe not that saved them. Because just
then an explosion boomed nearby, very close indeed. The
corridor shook, as if trying to shrug off the impact.
Konar's glance darted to the ceiling. Eddie's fist darted to
Konar's chin. The blow was not as powerful as the
missile, but it did its job just as well.

Cally didn't blink, either. A kick to her right, a fist to
her left. A third Diluvian opened fire but she was
ducking beneath the range of his weapon and ramming
into his stomach before he could readjust, doubling him

up, finishing him off with a further flurry of blows.

'Grab a gun!' Eddie was yelling. Konar looked like he might be considering raising himself from the floor. Eddie's foot persuaded him otherwise. 'Let's go. Kiri.' Grabbing her arm as she gazed down at the fallen Diluvians with a mixture of dread and loathing. 'Let's *go*.'

They went, quickly yet cautiously, without any real direction. Wherever they arrived had to be an improvement over where they'd been.

'There's never an exit sign when you need one,' Eddie grumbled.

'Eddie, we can't leave.' Cally pointed out what she had assumed was the obvious. 'We have to try to stop them launching their sun.'

'What, even though we're massively outnumbered and highly likely to be blown to smithereens by our own side's guns?' Eddie grinned. 'You're quite right, of course, Cal.' The grin slipped. 'But what about Kiri? We can't . . .'

'You can.' The Hawaiian girl spoke with surprising finality. 'You've no choice. *We've* no choice. If the Diluvians launch that sun then we'll have lost and my father will have died for nothing. Do what you need to do. I'll help as best I can.' She regarded the alien blaster in her hand strangely, ran her finger along its nozzle. 'I won't get in your way, I promise.'

Another explosion rocked the corridor. 'Okay,' said Eddie, 'then I reckon the first thing we need to do is get to a computer. Cal, it might be sensible to let Spy High know we're here.'

*

Ben yanked on his camouflage whites with almost vicious speed, the words of Senior Tutor Grant reverberating in his head. 'We must proceed on the assumption that Ben's premise is correct, and that the purpose of the Diluvians and Craven manufacturing an artificial sun here is to melt the ice-cap and bring chaos to the Earth's eco-system.' For once, it gave Ben no pleasure to be right, not when that probably meant the end of the world as he knew it. 'Even if this turns out not to be the case, we cannot leave such a potentially devastating weapon in the hands of our enemies. But neither can we simply destroy it. A stray missile could start a chain reaction in the sun that could end up doing the aliens' work for them. So we incapacitate it from the *inside*. That's your job, Bond Team.'

Ben glanced across at Jake who was also now clothed for arctic operations. It hadn't been Jake who'd raised the issue of how massively outnumbered Bond Team were going to be even if they managed to gain access to the fortress. Jake hadn't seemed to care.

But Grant had evidently given the matter some thought. 'Most of the enemy are human,' he'd noted, 'and while, as Technician Channing pointed out, Diluvian physiology is not in many respects the same as our own, we have a little something for you that might help equalise the odds.'

Ben checked the little something now. A variation circling his right forearm of the regulation Spy High sleepshot wrist-band, inlaid with what appeared to be tiny wire-mesh speakers. Filter plugs were fitted snugly in his ears. Deveraux technology always came up with an edge from somewhere, but Ben knew that in the end success or failure on a mission was the sole responsibility of the technology's *user*. It was the human factor that counted.

'You ready?' Ben called to Jake.

'Are you kidding?'

They joined the girls and descended to the spycopter's skimmer deck. Techs had the machines primed and ready to fly. Unexpectedly, Senior Tutor Grant was also there. Even more unexpectedly, given the gravity of the present circumstances, he seemed to be smiling.

'Some news you ought to be aware of,' he said. 'Good news.'

'The Diluvians have given up and gone home?' Bex hoped. 'Craven's surrendered?'

'Cally and Eddie are alive.'

'What?' Disbelief and delight. Relief on the face of Bex in particular. And Lori – was it wrong that she felt grateful that there had still been no casualties during her tenure as team leader? She found her voice: 'How do you know?'

'They're inside the fortress,' supplied Grant. 'They just signalled their personal identification codes to Deveraux. No further communication than that, I'm afraid, but at least we know you have allies. Locate them if you can, though the mission must take priority.' A chorus of 'Yes, sirs'. 'And if you do find them, they'll need these.' Grant handed two further sets of filter plugs to Lori which she sealed in her belt-pouch. 'Extra blasters, as well. And once again, good luck.'

Bex winced. 'Let's hope luck's something we *don't* need.'

❖

Lori felt her stomach heave and her vision blur as her skimmer disengaged from the spycopter and dropped silently to the arctic wastes below. The machines were as white as their pilot's garb, even down to the steel poles that held the shell together, so they'd be hard for the fortress' defenders to spot. But this was still the most dangerous part of the flight. If they were seen and targeted before the skimmers could reach their optimum operational height scant metres from the ground, it was doubtful their weaponry could cope with the kind of hardware at the Diluvians' disposal. Grant had instructed a second feigned assault to coincide with the skimmers' launch, hopefully to distract attention from Bond Team. Lori prayed the plan would work.

She remembered their disaster in the desert. Not auspicious. But practice was one thing. A live mission was quite another.

She saw the fortress raked with machine-gun fire, nothing that would penetrate its unyielding walls or threaten the artificial sun within. Crackshot pilots were suddenly starting to miss their mark. The diversion was well under way.

Now for their part. Lori gunned the skimmer's engine while its nose was still pointing directly to the ice. She could see her craft's shadow rising to meet her, black like a grave. She'd better get the split in split-second-timing right or she'd be taking no further part in this operation or any other. And Bond Team would be looking for a third leader.

At the last moment Lori reared her machine up, activated the automatic stabilisers. Her acceleration now was taking her directly towards the fortress. The snow and ice dipped and rose unevenly below her, gullies, crevasses, but the ground on which the Diluvians had built was solid enough, good for a landing. She was close enough too to make out the individual panels in the great block of steel ahead, the gunports spitting death, anti-aircraft fire from the roof, doors set into the base. Lori didn't need to remind her flanking team-mates of what to do next.

They skidded their skimmers to a halt on the snow, released themselves from the safety straps. Shock blasters to the fore, eyes scouring the fortress in case their approach had been witnessed. Seemed not.

Bond Team hastened to the fortress wall, flattened themselves against it. Now only an unfeasibly perpendicular shot from the structure's defenders could harm them, and they still seemed very much occupied with the air assault. As Bex gazed up, she saw one attack helicopter caught by Diluvian fire, watched it explode, the rotors crumple like burning leaves, saw it fireball spiralling to the hard, cold earth. Nobody got out. If she needed any further resolve, she had it then.

'Door,' Jake urged. 'Lori.'

'Deactivator no good,' Lori frowned. 'No apparent locking mechanism. Must only be operated from inside.'

'Who cares?' Jake took Lori's place closest to the door. 'More than one way to skin a cat.' He selected a small wedge of what looked like putty from his belt, tore it into four and pressed the pieces to each of the door's four edges. He worked quickly, economically. Exposure to the air was already making the substance smoulder.

He had about ten seconds. 'Door looks too thick for nitro-nails.'

'And we don't have time for explanations,' Ben said. 'Get back, Jake.'

Jake got back. All four Bond Teamers averted their eyes. The door exploded.

'Knock knock,' grinned Jake.

They entered in pairs, stealthily yet speedily, Ben and Bex on one side of the corridor, Lori and Jake on the other. No immediate opposition, but the Diluvians had to know there'd been a breach in their security.

'Pity we had to announce ourselves so soon,' reflected Lori.

'Priorities, Lo,' Jake said. 'Like staying alive.'

A handful of Craven's men were charging towards them, a movement at least temporarily halted by a fusillade of stun blasts from Bond Team's shock blasters. Bex's right hand was busy with her contribution, but her left hand was drawn towards the new wrist-band that all of them wore.

'No.' Ben advised her to resist the temptation. 'Later, Bex, when we're more central. We can finish these guys off without it.'

'You think?' Bex wondered why there never seemed to be sufficient cover in a corridor. 'Do the words Pinned and Down not mean anything to you?' Laser bolts blistered the floor at her feet.

'Do the words Cally and Eddie mean anything to *you*?' Ben parried.

Suddenly their team-mates were there, falling on Craven's men from behind. A combination of fists and stun blasts brought the little confrontation to a close.

'Eddie!' From everybody. 'Cal!'

'Hi, guys. What kept you?'

Rather different body language now, hugs swapped for blows and smiles for scowls. Ben and Cally. Bex and, much to his surprise, Eddie.

'I knew you weren't dead,' Bex said.

'I knew I wasn't, as well,' Eddie quipped. And it was good that Bex seemed interested, or was she just cosying up to him out of guilt? 'Sadly, the same can't be said of our old friend Oliver Craven.'

'Craven's dead?' Lori gaped.

'He's not moving and he's got kind of a big hole in his chest, so I reckon yeah,' diagnosed Eddie. 'As a dodo.'

'He deserved it. He had my father killed.' For the first time, Kiri Ho drew attention to her presence.

Eddie introduced her quickly.

'Yeah. Hi,' said Jake, 'but can the social niceties wait? We've got Diluvians to deal with. Give them their blasters.'

'You know about the Diluvians?' Cally marvelled.

'Sure,' winked Ben. 'We're Bond Team, aren't we? We know everything.'

'A pity that knowledge will do you no good.' Diluvians, maybe half a dozen of them. Weapons trained on the teenagers. Lori cursed herself for her laxness. Here they were in the enemy's base and she'd allowed the team to let their guard down. Amateur! If it wasn't so vital for the world that they should defeat the aliens, they deserved to fail. 'Drop your guns!'

'Drop them? But I've only just been given mine.' Eddie was grudging, but like the rest of his team-mates, he had little choice but to comply.

'Konar,' recognised Cally.

'I see you are already acquainted,' the Diluvian observed. 'Perhaps you are friends. In which case I would prepare to say your farewells. Take them to Krynor.'

FIVE

Bond Team bunched together as the Diluvians herded them towards the heart of the fortress. They made no attempt to overpower their guards, partly because the aliens were now in possession not only of their own firearms but of the shock blasters too, and partly because they were being taken where secretly they longed to go. The tables were all set and laid and ready to be turned.

Lori drifted close to Cally. 'They're building a sun,' she whispered.

'We've seen it. They're going to melt —'

'In their dreams.' Lori's fingers delved into her belt-pouch, found Cally's hand. 'You'll need these. You'll know when.'

Cally nodded. Lori increased her pace to catch up with Eddie. 'You know, you really don't have to be with us,' he was explaining to a Diluvian. 'I know my own way to the control room from here.' The guard was not impressed. He wasn't very attentive either, as Lori slipped a second set of filter plugs into Eddie's palm.

If only life had time-outs, Ben was thinking, like in a

football game. There were things he wanted to say to Cally that he didn't want to have to keep back until after the mission's completion, things he wanted to say in case they didn't *make* the mission's completion, and he guessed it was pretty much the same with Eddie and Bex. But there was no time, no chance. Spies in the field had no private lives, no past and no future. The immediate was all that could be allowed to matter.

And they'd reached the control room already.

'What's this?' Krynor actually managed to look surprised. '*More* of those interfering human children. Is your race not capable of sending warriors to defend itself? Even your war machines act with the weakness of cowards.' Viewscreens showed the air assault in full retreat. Biding their time, Lori knew.

'It doesn't need anybody older than us to deal with scum like you,' snorted Jake. 'By the way, your friends in the spaceship send their regards. Afraid they're unable to be here themselves. As for your ship, can you still claim on insurance after a self-destruct?'

'You were responsible for that?' Krynor said with malignant interest. 'Well, well.' Krynor smiled sadistically. 'Then I have something very special in store for you.'

'Funny,' said Jake. 'I was just about to say the same thing.'

'Now!' yelled Lori.

Four fingers stabbed at wrist-bands in perfect synchronicity. Not sleepshot this time. Sound. From the wire-mesh speakers of Bond Team's sonic blasters a high-pitched wail ripped through the air, shredding it like knives through paper. Cally and Eddie instantly pressed their filter plugs into their ears to immunise them from the sonic scream, but just as instantly, every human in the control room who lacked similar protection was clawing at their ears in writhing agony, twisting from their computer consoles as though riddled with bullets, crying out, incapacitated. No further threat.

Like lightning, Bond Team flashed into action to make the same true of the Diluvians, karate blows to disable arms, pressure points targeted with paralysing accuracy. The aliens' hearing might have been different enough to spare them the pain of the sonic blasters, but their physical form was sufficiently human for Bond Team to deprive it of consciousness with ruthless efficiency. 'Mine, I think,' growled Jake, snatching his shock blaster back from one reeling alien.

Yet there was a gap in the teenagers' otherwise united front. Kiri had no filter plugs. It was as if daggers were gouging out her eardrums. She was screaming, doubling up. Eddie had rushed to her side. He was holding her, helpless to do anything else. And if he was with Kiri, he wasn't taking out an opponent.

Krynor saw the opening and exploited it. He lunged towards them. Eddie saw him coming, belatedly assumed a defensive posture. Too little and too late. Krynor's fist clubbed the side of Eddie's head, almost drove the filter plug into his skull. Eddie sprawled to the ground, rolled, struggling to see straight. His vision cleared in time to see Krynor grabbing Kiri's arm and yanking her with him, covering fire from Konar allowing the two Diluvians to escape from the control room with their hostage intact.

'Kiri . . .' Eddie staggered to his feet. 'They can't . . . I'm coming . . .'

He lurched, nearly fell. Bex was there to hold him steady. 'No, you're not,' she said.

'Bit of a problem . . . with the old balance. I'll be fine . . . really . . .'

'Sit him down,' Lori was saying. 'Put his head between his knees.'

'Sounds . . . good . . .'

Lori looked about her. Senseless Diluvians and groaning henchmen littered the floor. 'Sonics off,' she instructed. 'I think they've done their job. Jake, Ben, guard the door. Anyone turns up with blue skin and no ears, stun them.' She activated her belt communicator. 'Sir? We've secured the control room. We've also found Cally and Eddie alive and well.'

'Though I'm gonna have,' moaned Eddie, 'a splitting headache.'

Senior Tutor Grant's voice replied to Lori. 'Have Cally override and immobilise the fortress' automated defence systems.'

'On it,' said Cally, seating herself at a console.

'We'll be with you as soon as possible,' Grant continued. 'Without humans to bolster their forces, the Diluvians won't keep us long.'

'What about the sun?' Lori asked.

'Close it down. Get Cally on to it as soon as she's disabled the defences.'

'All this work,' Cally protested good-humouredly. 'Any chance of a rise?'

'All this banter. Any chance of rescuing Kiri?' Eddie stood. This time he didn't sway or totter. 'And I don't want to sound like a party pooper, but Konar and Krynor aren't exactly under lock and key either.'

'I'm afraid they'll have to wait,' Lori said. 'Kiri, too.'

'Huh?' Eddie cupped his right ear forward. 'Maybe Krynor hit me harder than I thought, Lo, but you didn't just say they'd have to wait, did you?'

'I'm afraid I did, Ed.'

'What? So they've got plenty of time to murder Kiri like they did her father? This what you call a leadership decision, is it?'

Lori winced. It sounded harsh and unfeeling, she knew. 'The objectives of the mission have to take priority, Eddie.'

'That's a textbook talking.' Eddie wasn't happy. 'You turn into Ben when nobody was looking?'

'What's that supposed to mean, Nelligan?' Now Ben wasn't happy either.

'Lori's leader, Eddie,' Jake reminded him brusquely. 'You do what she says or we might just fall out.'

'So what if the rest of you stay here if you want and I try and track Kiri down myself? We *owe* her. We can't just abandon her.'

'I'll go with you, Eddie,' volunteered Bex.

'No, you *won't*.' Lori's voice was uncharacteristically steely. 'Nobody's going anywhere just yet and nobody's abandoning anyone *ever*. We all stay here until Cally's done her job and then we deal with Krynor. I'm sorry, Eddie. That's the way it's got to be.'

'Well, take your marks, guys and gals,' Cally grinned. 'Defence systems are very definitely offline.' Her lithe fingers blurred across the keyboard. 'I'll just do the same for the Diluvians' sun and . . .'

'What? *What?*' Ben called. Unfinished sentences in the field usually meant problems.

'Computer's unable to access any of the sun's engineering or control systems. We've been shut out from within the launch silo itself.'

'You mean someone's in there?' Lori said.

'Soon find out, as long as I can still activate the monitor screen.'

She could. The silo flickered into view, what little of it could be glimpsed behind the form of Commander Krynor. Konar was there, too, some further Diluvians who must have joined them along the way, and one other person. 'Kiri!' Eddie saw her, still barely conscious after the sonic blast, Konar pinning her arms to her sides.

Krynor was aware that he was being observed, and by whom. He took his gun, displayed it to his unseen audience, pressed its muzzle almost tenderly against Kiri's forehead. 'No!' Eddie cried. He was clawing at the screen. Krynor was laughing. His arm suddenly swung round. His weapon fired. Eddie instinctively flinched back.

The monitor screen went black. Not even Cally would be able to fix that.

'They've got her,' Eddie said. 'They've still got her.'

'And she's alive,' Lori added.

'Yeah, but for how long?'

'All the while they think that keeping her alive might deter us from attacking them,' assumed Bex.

'Well, they're not leaving in a hurry,' Lori said. 'Maybe we'd better wait for Grant to get here before we decide our next move.'

'Maybe we'd better not.' Cally indicated a counter that had suddenly come alive. The hour that it had initially registered was already now reduced by seconds. 'I think Krynor's sun is about to rise.'

'But if he's in the silo he'll be burned to a crisp,' Bex winced.

'I doubt he cares,' Lori reasoned. 'Not if it means the Diluvians triumph. And if that sun buries itself in the ice-cap, that's what it will mean.'

'Yeah, and there won't be much left of Kiri, either, Ms Nobody's Abandoning Anyone.' Eddie glared at Lori accusingly.

'Okay.' Lori ran her hands through her hair. 'Then let's do something about it, shall we?'

She crawled through the ventilation duct and fought to keep her mind on the matter at hand. In less than a minute she and Jake would have reached the grille that permitted access to the silo. Then there'd be abseiling to deal with, maddened Diluvians, a race to save the planet.

And here Lori was agonising over whether she was really cut out to be a leader.

It seemed to her that one moment the emotional strain was all too much for her and she was on the point of resignation, as when they'd believed Eddie and Cally to be lost, while the next she was being too emotion*less*, almost brutal with her decisions, as over Kiri just now. She'd been forced to argue with Eddie – *Eddie*, of all people, Mr Chilled. She was going to have to find a better balance in her new role if she was going to make it work.

Eddie and Bex were at that very second scrambling through the ventilation duct's twin on the other side of the silo. But he shouldn't have been there. As he and Cally weren't fully equipped for active operations, Lori's original teamings had the two of them blasting the door to the silo while the others penetrated via the ducts that the fortress plans had disclosed. Eddie had pretty much refused. 'No' was pretty much a refusal, however you tried to dress it up. He wanted to get to Kiri; Kiri was his responsibility. And Lori had given in. Luckily, Ben had been happy to go with Cally, willing to loan his belt and sleepshot wrist-band to Eddie, but that didn't silence the nagging doubts in Lori's mind. She'd allowed her original decision to be changed due to emotional pressure from a team-mate. Was that a sign of strength or weakness?

The grille that confronted her now provided no answers, but it did at least force her to focus.

'Okay, we're in position,' she whispered to Jake. Why the whisper she wasn't sure. The duct was some thirty metres above the silo's circular platform. Through the grille she could just about make out the figures of the Diluvians and Kiri Ho moving below her, some of them working at control panels. Smoke was rising beyond the shielding where the artificial sun was waiting to be launched into the arctic sky. The Prometheus Project would have supplied it with an anti-gravity propulsion unit that would have kept it hanging there for the benefit of those it warmed. The Diluvians, Lori guessed, had omitted that aspect of Elleray's design and replaced it with a directional guidance system that would aim the blazing satellite at the polar ice-cap like a fiery bomb. The consequences of *that* would be incalculable.

Lori produced a laser cutter from her belt, went to work on the grille. Jake shuffled alongside. 'Two laser cutters are better than one,' he grinned.

'Eddie? Bex?' Lori used the communicator. 'How are things with you?'

'We're at the grille,' Eddie's voice returned. 'Cutting through now.'

'Good. Wait for my word.'

'Word had better be quick,' Eddie muttered, slicing through the obstructive metal with the relish of a psychotic surgeon.

Bex watched him with a degree of nervousness that surprised her, kind of first-date nervousness. 'So you and this Kiri girl got pretty close while you were in Hawaii?' she said.

'Kind of,' Eddie replied, without the traditional wisecrack. 'Put it this way, if it wasn't for me and Cal, Kiri's life wouldn't be in danger.'

'We'll save her, Ed, don't worry,' Bex assured him. Even if Kiri *was* a potential rival.

In the corridor outside the silo, Cally and Ben faced a very sealed door, appearing impregnable, its rivets jutting out into the corridor like a boxer's chin. The Bond Teamers were covering both directions with shock blasters, just waiting for the order from Lori to blow the door. They only hoped that their explosives would be equal to the task.

'Surprised you didn't want to scramble through the ventilation system with Bex,' Cally fished. 'Dropping in on the enemy's your sort of thing, isn't it, Ben?'

'I don't know. I reckon blowing things up with you could get to be my sort of thing as well, Cal.'

'The Big Bang theory of relationships, huh?'

Cally might have said more but for Lori's voice suddenly issuing from her belt communicator. Both other teams were ready. It was time to blow the door.

The banter immediately ceased. Cally and Ben tore open packets of the putty-like material that Jake had used to breach the fortress itself. As he'd done, they pressed it to the door and stepped smartly aside. Within seconds, they'd be through. As the explosives reacted with oxygen, smouldered, detonated. As the blast shook the corridor. Within seconds, they'd be inside the silo with their team-mates.

Or not.

Cally and Ben stared at each other in dismay. The door was dented, damaged, but it was not destroyed.

Commander Krynor of the Diluvian Advance Guard heard the explosion, saw the weighty silo door buckle, and knew what it meant. 'The human children seek entry,' he scowled. 'Deny them!' He gestured everyone apart from Konar and those of his race working on the sun's launch controls towards the door.

Which only went to prove that even Commanders of the Diluvian Advance Guard could make mistakes. That was exactly what Lori had wanted him to do.

In the commotion, nobody looked up. Nobody saw the grilles of the ventilation ducts removed, the potentially betraying white of Spy High arctic camouflage suits as Bond Team prepared to abseil in.

Lori released her belt-line and affixed the pad on the end of the wire to the duct's roof. She pulled hard on it. The line didn't budge – impregnated with the same adhesive as clingskin.

Jake followed suit. 'Ladies first, though?'

'Ladies nothing,' said Lori. 'Leaders. The word is *go*, people.'

Lori and Eddie pitched themselves backwards from the ducts on either side of the silo, leaping into thin and increasingly humid air, the tensile wire of their belt-lines controlling their descent, swinging them back towards the silo wall. One hand on the wire to assist balance, the other firmly gripping the handle of a shock blaster to assist survival, that was how they'd been taught. That was how they did it now.

Maybe Eddie had been dozing when they'd also been taught not to announce their presence until it was unavoidable, because his blaster was blazing even before Jake and Bex had exited the ducts.

'Behind us! Kill them!' Krynor rapidly readjusted his strategy.

Lori and Eddie disengaged their belt-wires, left them dangling and darted for cover, forced the Diluvians to shoot at them rather than at the easier targets of the abseiling Jake and Bex. From mid-air Jake fired not at the aliens but at the flickering computer wall that was busily activating the artificial sun. He hit something important, that was for sure, but not quite what he'd hoped.

The silo's protective plastiglass shielding began to lower. The platform on which human and Diluvian fought now became a precipice as the smoke and the heat of the raging inferno below rolled over the desperate combatants in suffocating waves.

It was cooler in the corridor outside. And possible to think.

Cally was firing her shock blaster at the panelling of the walls on either side of the door, stripping it away.

'You want to tell me why?' Ben said.

'So we can't blast through the door directly,' Cally explained. 'So let's go *around* it.'

'Through the walls?' As the metal skin was flayed, Ben saw the interior workings of circuits and wires, like bloodless veins.

'Not quite. The door's mechanisms have got to be electronic. Let's see what happens if we disrupt the power supply.'

She fired again. In a shower of sparks, severed wires writhed like decapitated snakes. The defiant door was defeated at last. And from the sights and sounds of battle now exposed to Cally and Ben as it slid compliantly open, not a moment too soon.

Lori shouted with delight as the sudden and intensely welcome appearance of her final pair of team-mates created a cross-fire that even the warrior Diluvians would find it difficult to elude. No time for any of them to monitor the controls now. In a circle around Krynor, they had other things on their minds.

One by one, as shock blasts struck them, the aliens spun and fell.

They'd be threatening to kill Kiri any second now, Eddie knew, as soon as they realised they were losing. It was inevitable. And Lori wouldn't be able to allow the mission to fail, the sun to be launched, for the life of one girl. That was inevitable, too. So he'd better do something about it himself.

Konar still held a struggling Kiri close to him, but he was also at a little distance from his remaining companions. If he reached them, it could be game over for Kiri.

'Cover me!' Eddie snapped to Bex, was up and

running without waiting for a reply, hurtling across the platform, crouching low, ignoring Diluvian fire that stung and singed the metal at his feet. Konar grinning, aimed his weapon at Eddie. At point-blank range the blast would probably go right through him and then he wouldn't have to worry about Kiri any more. He threw himself forward and at Konar's legs as the blast scorched over his head. He rammed into the alien whose knees were popping like they were broken, knocked him hard to the floor, clear of his weapon and, more vitally, Kiri. Konar's hairless skull cracked against the metal surface. Both were hard, but the platform was harder.

Any self-congratulation in which Eddie might have been tempted to indulge was going to have to be postponed. A Diluvian boot caught him above the temple. He rolled with the blow as always, was aware of a shape above him, that seemed to want to trample him. Eddie rolled but he could scarcely breathe from the heat. He felt like he was being boiled alive and he'd better not roll any further.

His leg kicked out over empty space. It was like he'd thrust it into a blast furnace. The platform ended here and beyond was only a plunge into the sun. But the figure towered over him.

It was Krynor. Krynor with a gun.

At least he might have saved Kiri.

'At least I'll kill *you*,' snarled the Diluvian Commander.

Nothing that Eddie could do. The sound of a shot.

No pain.

And Krynor, puzzled, staggering forward. Krynor dropping his weapon. Toppling over Eddie, over the lip of the platform. Krynor still able to scream as he pitched headlong towards the fruit of the Prometheus Project, but it didn't last for long. Like the rest of him, it went up in smoke.

'Who?' Eddie groped to his feet. The final Diluvians were surrendering, covered by Lori and Jake. Cally and Ben were at the launch controls – looked like there'd still be snow at the North Pole for Christmas. And Bex, crouched in pain, nursing a wounded arm, her firing arm. So who had shot Krynor?

And then Eddie saw who. She was standing frozen, fixed in the moment of firing. She'd used Konar's gun. And Kiri Ho's eyes were wide with the magnitude of what she'd done.

SIX

'It was good of Senior Tutor Grant to let us use his study, wasn't it?' said Eddie, inviting Kiri to sit and make herself comfortable.

'I don't understand what for.' Kiri took the chair, but she looked far from comfortable. Her eyes roamed the room nervously.

'I guess he thought we could do with a little quiet time together, before you go back to Hawaii. Spy High might be a lot of things, but private it ain't.' Eddie led with a smile, but Kiri didn't follow. Instead she looked down at her hands, her right hand particularly, which she seemed to be regarding with a mix of horror and distrust. It was the hand that had held the gun. Eddie pretended not to notice. 'He's even left us something to drink,' he said. 'You want some, Kiri?'

A listless shrug he interpreted as a yes, which was probably just as well. With a heavy heart, Eddie poured the cordial from jug into glass, offered it to Kiri.

'So what do you think of the place anyway? Is it what you expected?'

'I suppose so. I'm not really sure.' The enthusiasm that Kiri had once expressed to visit Spy High, to play an active part in the Deveraux College, seemed not to have survived the Diluvians. She sipped her drink distantly. 'I'm not really sure I took in what you showed me, Eddie. All I seem to be able to see is Krynor falling, and the gun in my hand as I kill him. That's all I dream about as well, every night since the fortress. I hate it.'

'You saved my life, Kiri,' Eddie pointed out gently. 'And what Krynor was planning to do . . .'

'I know. I know. You can tell me that. You all *have* told me that.' Kiri gazed almost pleadingly at Eddie. 'And part of me had wanted revenge for my father as well, but that part of me was wrong. I don't feel any better now. I don't feel good or justified in what I did, even if I should. I feel bad. I feel dirty. I feel like nothing I do makes sense any more.'

'I can understand that,' Eddie soothed.

'Can you? I doubt it. You and the others, all of the students here, you've *chosen* to become part of a world that thrives on danger, where death is an everyday occurrence, a routine that you've grown used to and accept, that you've come to expect. I can't live like that, Eddie. I thought when we first met that I could be like you, that I *was* like you, but I'm not. Spy High frightens me. What you do frightens me.' The tears stung her eyes. 'My dad's dead and I just want to go home.'

'Kiri.' Eddie spoke her name sadly. 'Are you sure? Is that what you really want?'

'No.' Kiri smiled bitterly. 'What I really want is never to have seen you. Or Cally. Eddie, it's nothing personal. What I really want is for Dad never to have been a

Selector Agent, for none of this ever to have happened.
But that's not likely, is it?'

'No,' said Eddie quietly. 'It's not likely. Drink up,
though.'

'What is this anyway?' Kiri puzzled at the cordial as if
it was some kind of magic potion. 'Tastes good, but
strange.'

'Special Spy High recipe,' Eddie said.

'Not having any yourself?'

'No.' His expression was sad. 'No need.'

'No . . . need . . .?' Her voice was slurring, drifting.

'I want to thank you, Kiri,' Eddie said, 'while you can
still hear me. Thank you for saving my life. I'll always
remember you. Be happy.'

'. . . Eddie . . .'

'Bye.'

And he took the glass from her unprotesting fingers as
Kiri slumped back into her chair and slept. Bent forward
to kiss her brow.

'You can come in now, sir,' he said.

Senior Tutor Grant did. He was accompanied by two
techs. 'We'll take over now, Eddie,' he said. 'You did a
good job.'

Eddie sighed. 'Is it right, though, Sir? We mind-wipe
Kiri, we send her back to Hawaii, she wakes up and
learns that her father's died in a boat accident. We
reshape her past as we see fit. How *can* it be right?'

'I know what you mean, Eddie,' said Grant, running
his hands through his hair, 'but we have no other choice.
If we allowed Kiri to retain her memories of us, of the
Diluvians and Craven, given her state of mind she could
possibly prove to be a danger both to herself and to the

integrity of Deveraux. The importance of our work renders such a prospect unacceptable.'

'What about the value of truth, though, sir?' said Eddie.

'In our business, Eddie,' Grant said soberly, 'truth is always the servant of necessity.'

So it was another triumph for Bond Team, Eddie pondered as he paced the floor of his, Ben and Jake's room. The others were fortunately elsewhere at the moment. Another great victory over the enemies of peace, freedom, democracy, Mom's apple pie, etc, etc. The Bond Team boys (and girls, naturally) had done good. And realistically Eddie supposed they had. The threat to the ice-cap had been averted, Prometheus technology redirected to the beneficial use that Douglas Elleray had intended, Craven was dead, Krynor crisped and the surviving Diluvians, their salvageable technology, their knowledge of the faraway bits of the cosmos, all now at Deveraux's and the authorities' other secret agencies' command. They'd even been able to broadcast a message in Diluvian to the fleet out there in space suggesting that they might want to consider looking elsewhere for their next conquest because if they ventured too close to Earth they'd go the same way as their Advance Guard. What was all that if not a happy ending?

So how come Eddie felt like he'd just seen his first love in a clinch with his best friend? Truth and necessity, Grant had said. Did he mean it wasn't necessary to think about the innocent casualties of the mission, Ken Ho, Douglas Elleray, all those people at Solartech and in Littleport? Sure, more would have died if the Diluvians hadn't been stopped, *countless* more, but the head didn't always master the heart. Eddie still *felt* for those who were gone. Maybe he was closer to Kiri Ho than she'd thought, only better at covering it up with quips, one-liners and a reputation for taking nothing seriously.

Too late, though, now. He'd never see Kiri again. She didn't even know that Eddie Nelligan existed. But maybe it was for the best. It was probably foolish to imagine that he could have a relationship with any girl who didn't know about his life at Spy High or couldn't cope with it. Trouble was, that rather narrowed his field. Lori was *definitely* spoken for, Cally on the way, it seemed, and as for . . .

A knock on the door, tentative and tremulous.

'Come on in,' Eddie called. 'I'm not naked.'

'Glad to hear it.' Bex opened the door, stood in the doorway like it was the edge of a cliff and she was scared of falling. 'Hi, Eddie.'

'Bex?' Too surprised, too high-pitched. 'I mean, Bex.' Better. Lower. More manly. He saw what she was holding but feigned ignorance. 'What are they?'

Flowers in the right hand. Chocolates in the left. 'Didn't know which you'd prefer,' Bex echoed Eddie's own words, 'so I brought both. And one other thing.'

'Not his and hers nose studs, is it?'

'An apology. I'm sorry, Eddie.' Bex gazed at him sincerely. 'The way I treated you before, it was wrong. You didn't deserve it. I *do* like you. When we thought you and Cal were, well, you know, I realised it. I like you. Maybe, if you want, we could find out how much. But I mean, you know, if you've changed your mind . . .'

Eddie grinned.

EPILOGUE

Graduation Day. The Deveraux College's grandest spectacle and greatest deception of the year. There were marquees in the grounds and fine wines flowing. The college's rooms and facilities were open for inspection, though not all the rooms and only some of the facilities. Up to a hundred invited guests, including the parents and families of this year's graduate students milled around, making small talk, praising their children, admiring the views and never guessing that Spy High lay only metres beneath their new-shoed feet, never imagining what their sons and daughters had *really* done to deserve their diplomas. And if any of them *did* gain an inkling, however accidentally, a little mind-wiping therapy was always available.

'I bet Grant's hoping there won't be an international crisis today,' Ben observed. 'It wouldn't look good if in the middle of the ceremony the entire school had to run out of the hall, jump on SkyBikes and jet off to save the world.'

'Me, I'm kind of hoping we do,' complained Eddie. 'It'll give me an excuse to get out of these clothes.' Bond Team were already regaled in the traditional gowns and mortar-boards of graduation ceremonies. They were gathered in the girls' room. 'I mean, I keep stepping on this stupid gown thing and as for this crazy hat, I bet it looks great on guys with square, flat heads. But me, it's like trying to balance a book on the top of your head.'

'And you've always been pretty *un*balanced, right, Ed?' Bex laughed, but affectionately now, and she wasn't standing next to Eddie by coincidence.

'Well, I think we'd better be making our way down-stairs,' said Lori. 'The parents'll be here soon.'

'Those that are coming,' Jake scowled. 'Those that can be bothered.' The last he'd heard, the farm was still an inescapable ball and chain around his family's collective leg.

'You never know, Jake.' Lori squeezed his hand encouragingly.

'I do know,' Jake said.

Cally felt like saying, at least your parents *can* come, but it wasn't Jake's fault that hers were either dead or far away, not caring about the child they'd brought into the world sixteen years ago. One day, maybe she ought to employ Spy High's resources to try to track her parents down, discover the truth about her background once and for all, but one day wasn't today. And what if she didn't like what she found?

The others were already at the door. Ben waited for her. 'Cal, come on,' he said. 'You can talk to *my* parents, if you can stand it.'

Cally wasn't sure she could. Mr and Mrs Stanton's smiles when they greeted her were just a little too stretched and pearly to be entirely genuine. Or maybe it was just the dental remodifications they'd both had done that were false.

'Cally. Of course.' Mrs Stanton. 'Didn't you come to Benjamin's birthday party? Of course you did. Now you must tell me, is 'Cally' short for anything?'

Mr Stanton steered Ben to one side in a father-to-son chat sort of way. 'Now where's that nice Lori, Ben, hey? This Cally seems a very nice girl, too, don't get me wrong, but your mother and I thought that you and Lori . . . I know the two of you have had some little disagreements lately, but I'm sure you can work them out . . .'

'The disagreements weren't exactly *little*, Dad,' Ben said, 'and we did resolve them. We split up. Lori's over there' – directing his father's attention to the other side of the marquee where Lori was introducing Jake to a pair of adults whose blondness alone suggested kinship – 'with her parents and Jake. Jake's Lori's boyfriend now, Dad, and I've got used to it. I think you and Mum are going to have to, as well.'

'Jake?' Mr Stanton's lips crinkled at the edges. 'At your party, didn't you say he was at Deveraux on a scholarship from the domes?' Mr Stanton's assessment of Lori's judgement seemed to be taking a turn for the worse. 'Oh, dear.'

Jake noticed Ben's father looking across at them and interpreted his slightly pained expression appropriately. He thought maybe he ought to give Mr Stanton a wave or something, or wipe his nose on his sleeve, just to confirm his inbred vulgarity, but that wouldn't have been fair to the new, post-leadership Ben, and more than that, Lori wouldn't have liked it. Though Lori herself seemed kind of nervous, glancing around as if she was expecting to see someone who hadn't appeared yet.

'Listen,' she finally said to him. 'Can you keep my parents company for a bit? I've got to pop out.'

'Sure,' he replied. 'What's going on, Lo?'

'You'll see.'

Mr and Mrs Angel asked polite questions that Jake answered on automatic. Spy High students had been so thoroughly trained in what responses to give about the school to members of the general public that he delivered his lines like a performance after countless rehearsals.

And he kept an eye open for Lori's return, too. Saw Eddie and Bex with a very tall, thin, red-haired man and a very short, squat dark-haired woman, the physical mismatch between them explaining a lot about their son. There was a good deal of laughter coming from that direction.

And Lori coming from the other. 'Sorry, Mum, Dad.' She seemed out of breath. Her eyes were shining. 'I need to borrow Jake if that's okay? I'll be back in a minute.' In case of refusal, she grabbed his hand and pulled.

They dashed out of the marquee, holding their mortar-boards to prevent them slipping off, their gowns flapping behind them. 'Will you tell me what's happening, Lo?' Jake demanded, verging towards annoyance. 'What's all this about?'

'Not what, Jake?' Lori laughed. '*Who.*'

And they were there. Impossibly. Making their way cautiously, uncertainly, from the school to the marquee. His father in the suit he reserved for special occasions only. His mother in a dress he'd never seen before and that looked new. His little sister Beth scrubbed and brushed and groomed as if she was going to church, one hand holding tightly on to the ragged dolls Peggy and Glubb, the other holding even more tightly to Mrs Daly's.

'Surprise,' Lori said.

'You can say that again.' Jake could hardly keep control of his voice. 'I mean, how? I don't . . .'

'I vidded your Mum,' said Lori. 'Thought if we had a little talk, and Beth, too, you know, all women together, we might be able to put a little pressure on your dad to change his mind. Looks like he did.'

'You can say that again,' Jake repeated. He was blinking, maybe because he didn't quite trust his eyes, maybe for some other reason.

'Sorry I didn't tell you, Jake, but if it didn't —'

'Hey, Lori.' He hugged her. 'You've got *nothing* to be sorry about. This is the best thing that could have happened to me today. I'll never forget it. I'll never forget that *you* made it possible.' He felt closer to her than to anyone. 'Anyway, guess I'd better go say hi to my family. They've come a long way.'

Lori watched him run towards them. Yeah, she thought. Haven't we all.

The ceremony was over. The newly graduated students had each filed up to the stage in the Presentation

Hall to be awarded their diplomas by Senior Tutor
Grant, Mr Jonathan Deveraux being unavoidably
detained elsewhere and having to miss the occasion.
Proud parents had applauded, perhaps the Dalys most
loudly of all. The year holograph had been taken on
the lawn, with the imposing gothic façade of the
Deveraux College towering behind. And to mark the
ending of the formal part of the day, with a collective
whoop of liberation the graduates had all thrown their
mortar-boards into the air. Eddie hadn't bothered to
catch his.

Bond Team were about to rejoin their families. 'You
reckon we can lose the gowns now, too?' Eddie was
saying. 'And I mean, like, literally. Maybe bury them
or something.'

'Do what you like, Ed,' said Jake. 'Me, I promised
I'd show my little sister the lake.'

'Sorry, Jake, but that's going to have to wait.' Senior
Tutor Grant had suddenly interposed himself between
the students and the marquee. 'Mr Deveraux would
like a word.'

Jake's initial protest died on his lips. You didn't say
no to a word with Mr Deveraux, not even if the presi-
dent of the United States wanted to be shown the lake.
Resentfully nonetheless, he followed the others inside
the accommodation wing and up to the special quarters
that housed the computerised mind of Jonathan
Deveraux.

The digitalised face of Jonathan Deveraux gazed
down at them from the screen like a god pleased with
his creation. Bex tried to kid herself that his eyes were
favouring her ahead of her team-mates, but she wasn't

easy to fool. As far as her late father was concerned, she was the same as Cally or Lori.

'On today of all days,' Jonathan Deveraux said, 'I wanted to congratulate you on the successful completion of your mission against Oliver Craven and the invaders. They may never know it, but the peoples of the world owe you a debt. You have more than fulfilled the rigorous standards required at the Deveraux College. Myself and your tutors are proud of you.'

A chorus of thank you, sirs.

'You have also opened our eyes to a possible new front in our ongoing war against terrorism and insanity, against those who would jeopardise the safe and peaceful future of our world. A front as limitless as space itself. We are now strengthening our lunar and satellite defences against possible incursions either by the Diluvians or any other hostile alien race. We are even developing a dedicated extra-terrestrial investigation and surveillance team to deal with any such dangers as they arise.

'However, whatever the threat, wherever it appears – from space or from here on Earth – I know you will be ready to confront, challenge, and ultimately defeat it for the good of all.'

And they thought about the Diluvians. They thought about Frankenstein and Talon and Nemesis and Drac. They thought about the risks they'd taken, the horrors they'd faced, the deaths they'd only narrowly escaped. They thought about Jennifer. But not one of them felt even the slightest desire to contradict Jonathan Deveraux. What he said was true.

Whatever the hazards tomorrow might bring, Lori, Jake, Cally, Ben, Eddie and Bex were ready and waiting. And they always would be.

SPY HIGH SERIES ONE ENDS HERE.
WANT MORE?
THEN LOOK OUT FOR . . .

EDWARD RED

The new Spy High novel from A. J. Butcher

Coming soon from Atom Books

www.atombooks.co.uk

About the Author

AJ Butcher has been aware of the power of words since avoiding a playground beating aged seven because he 'told good stories'. He's been trying to do the same thing ever since. Writing serial stories at school that went on forever gave him a start (if not a finish). A degree in English Literature at Reading University kept him close to books, while a subsequent career as an advertising copywriter was intended to keep him creative. As it seemed to be doing a better job of keeping him inebriated, he finally became an English teacher instead. His influences include Dickens and Orwell, though Stan Lee, creator of the great Marvel super-heroes, is also an inspirational figure. In his spare time, AJ reads too many comics, listens to too many '70s records and rants about politics to anyone who'll listen. When he was younger and fantasising about being a published author, he always imagined he'd invent a dashing, dynamic pseudonym for himself. Now that it's happened, however, he's sadly proven too vain for that. A. J. Butcher is his real and only name.

Have you read . . .

WAYWALKERS

by Catherine Webb

Sam Linnfer works part-time at a London university. He's a quiet chap with a real skill for tricksy ancient languages, and an affinity for cats. He's also immortal and the Son of Time. You might know him better as Lucifer. And with all the Gods in Heaven about to go to war over ownership of Earth, you're going to be extremely glad he's not *exactly* the person history portrays him to be.

In Catherine Webb's stunning new book, you'll come face to face with Jehovah on a cold Moscow night, walk the Ways between Earth and Heaven with Buddha, take a hair-raising cab ride with Adam (yes, the Adam – only he's into denim now, rather than fig-leaves!) and find yourself trusting the one person you never dreamed you could . . .

Because when the gods go to war and Earth is their battleground only the devil can save your soul

www.atombooks.co.uk

If you like great fantasy, you'll love . . .

FROM THE TWO RIVERS

Part One of The Eye of the World

by Robert Jordan

The Wheel turns and the greatest fantasy adventure of all time begins . . .

Life in Emond's Field has been pretty boring for Rand Al'Thor and his friends until a strange young woman arrives in their village. Moraine is an Aes Sedai, a magician with the ability to wield the One Power, and she brings warnings of a terrible evil awakening in the world. That very night, the village is attacked by blood-thirsty Trollocs – a fearsome tribe of beast-men thought to be no more than myth. As Emond's Field burns, Moraine and her warrior-guardian help Rand and his companions to escape. But it is only the beginning of their troubles. For Moraine believes Rand Al'Thor is the Dragon Reborn, and that he is fated to unite the world against the rising darkness and lead the fight against a being so powerful and evil it is known simply as *the Dark One*.

www.atombooks.co.uk

FOR MORE GREAT BOOKS LOOK OUT FOR THE ATOM LOGO . . .

WWW.ATOMBOOKS.CO.UK